ROCK HAP

Chris Spenc

This book is a work of fiction and is based on an original screenplay of the same name by Chris Spence and Kassra Nassiri.
Cover illustration by John Charles, 2021.

Table of Contents

For Kass Nassiri

Thanks for the musical inspiration and star-spangled guitar skills!

Prologue

San Francisco, California

Election Night

By the time he heard the sirens it was almost too late. Dr. John Locke's attention was so firmly fixed on his giant flatscreen it would probably have taken a bomb going off to distract him.

"As the results start to flood in it looks like a landslide for challenger Francesca Delano over the incumbent, President Donaldson," the television news anchor announced. "Exit polls show the public blaming the President for his handling of the economy and the pandemics, while warming to Francesca Delano's promise of a fairer deal for all Americans," she added.

The sirens were getting closer now, probably at the end of his street already. Still the sound barely registered in Dr. Locke's consciousness as he continued to stare at the television, his eyes flicking left-and-right as he followed the ticker tape of state-by-state exit polls across the bottom of the screen. Compared with what he was watching, a siren was not remotely important.

He was still absorbed in the election news when something odd happened. The television screen flickered for a second and the presenter looked momentarily confused, her eyes blinking once, then a second time as an odd, vacant expression crossed her face.

John Locke sat up in his chair, stroking his salt-and-pepper beard as his brows creased in concern.

"Excuse me," the news anchor said after several seconds' silence, her eyes more focused again. "So ... as I was saying, exit polls are calling a victory for incumbent President Donaldson over his radical challenger, Francesca Delano. It looks like the President's economic policies and handling of the pandemics have found favor with voters. Meanwhile, his opponent Francesca Delano's controversial ideas have evidently failed to win the public's confidence."

"What? No. They haven't ... they couldn't have," John Locke muttered to himself, staring in shock at the screen. "Did they just *steal* the election?"

"Yes, our pollsters are now prepared to call a surprising but decisive victory for President Donaldson, who secures a second term in office," the newscaster announced, suddenly smiling.

Smash!

Locke's head whipped around at the clang of metal striking metal. His brain belatedly registered the wail of the siren as he stood up and strode purposefully to the upper-floor window. Looking out onto the driveway below, he saw a large, military-style vehicle had crashed through the gates, wrenching one of them off its hinges and sending it flying onto the well-manicured lawns.

"*Sir, you have visitors*," came a robotic female voice from a device on the mahogany desk in the corner of the room.

"Thank you, Eleanor. It is the Patriotic Security Service. It seems my time here is at an end," he replied as half-a-dozen special forces poured out of the vehicle and started running towards the house, scanning it through infrared goggles, weapons held in readiness.

"*Should I initiate security measures, sir*?" the robotic voice asked.

"Yes please, Eleanor. And destroy all relevant records and electronic files on the mainframe, please."

"*Yes, sir. Good luck, sir.*"

Outside, the special ops troops, clad all in black, had fanned out and surrounded the building. The first reached for the front door handle but screamed and flew backwards as the door's defenses kicked in and a high-voltage blast of electricity surged through him. A second man trained his submachine gun on the door and rained bullets upon it, shredding the stout wood in seconds before kicking it open and bursting through. Meanwhile, a third soldier was breaking one of the windows and clambering over the sill, while a fourth had smashed down the back door, which was not electrified. He rushed through, only to find himself in darkness as the interior lights flickered, then blinked out. Confident his infrared goggles would give him the night vision he needed, he continued to advance quickly, but fell as an unseen tripwire caught him above the ankles, sending him sprawling to the ground. His finger inadvertently touched the hair trigger of his gun, spraying bullets across the corridor. A grunt from the darkness ahead was the only sign one of his comrades had been hit, a victim of friendly fire.

While his attackers were trying to enter the house, Dr. Locke had rushed to his desk, pulled open a draw and removed a slim folder containing a few dozen sheets of paper. He had headed downstairs and trotted towards the back of the house where a second set of steps led to an underground parking garage. Just seconds ahead of his pursuers, he had pulled open the door of his car, pausing for a moment at the sound of gunshots above. Looking over his shoulder at the dark stairway, he distractedly threw the folder onto the passenger seat, not noticing that a single sheet had slipped out and was now on the garage floor.

The soldiers' leader had now found her way to the top of the stairs leading down to the garage. She paused for a moment to listen, then sprinted forward, taking the steps two-at-a-time as she heard the deep-throated growl of a car engine.

She reached the underground garage just in time to see an unmarked SUV drive quickly up a ramp and towards a secret exit. Before she could raise her gun to fire, the car had rushed out into the night and around a corner.

"Update me, Captain," came a static-filled voice on the soldier's headset.

"He's escaped, General Arnold."

"Did you secure the documents?"

"No sign of any documents, General. And he appears to have wiped the databases," replied the soldier dismally, looking at a smoking mainframe computer in the corner of the room.

"Fool! I will not tolerate this type of failure!"

"Wait, General, I found something," she said, noticing the single sheet of paper on the ground. "I have a page here. There's something written on it," the soldier said hopefully.

She looked at the sheet. The number 42 was in the top right-hand corner. A page number, perhaps? If so, it must have been the end of the document, for the page itself contained only one short, handwritten sentence: *"Keep Alexander F. under observation."*

Did its brevity make it useless, the soldier wondered? And who was this "Alexander" anyway?

Chapter One
Fifteen Years Later
MeChip, Myself and I

Alexander Franklin was in his own world.

He was sitting on his bed holding his Happy Laser Six-String Mark 7, his brows creased in concentration. His right hand held a guitar pick between his thumb and two fingers as it strummed rhythmically, while the fingers of his left moved deftly from one position to another, always finding the right chords: G—F—G—E minor—C—B7—then back to G again. His mind, absorbed completely in his music and the sounds filling his headset, was utterly unaware of his surroundings, from the posters of famous musicians adorning the walls to the dirty socks and candy wrappers strewn across the rug.

Unaware not only of his surroundings, but also, apparently, of the time.

"Alexander! Breakfast, now!" came a shout from the other side of his door, accompanied by a sharp rapping. His mother's voice penetrated the music in his headset as Alex paused, checked the time and stood up, reluctantly placing his guitar on the bed.

"Okay, Mom, I'm coming!" he called back as he made his way to the bathroom.

Brushing his teeth, he frowned at his reflection in the mirror—his unruly mop of brown hair, blue eyes, and slender frame he wished was a bit bulkier. He returned to his room and pulled on his favorite chromo-jeans, pleth-boots, white t-shirt and retro-jacket, before heading downstairs with his backpack and guitar, now stowed lovingly in its case. His father had already left for work and, since Alex had no brothers or sisters, only his mother remained in the house. She was busying herself in the kitchen, evidently trying to get out in a hurry.

"Come on Alex, eat up! We have to go in five minutes," she said, not looking up from the table where she was pushing piles of papers into a small satchel.

Alex didn't answer, but sat down and started shoveling cereal into his mouth. He was, in fact, already watching his favorite music show, Rock Shop Hero, which he'd called up onto his retina using his MeChip. While the kitchen was still faintly visible, it had faded into the background as Rock Shop Hero came into the front of his vision.

"Did you remember the field trip form?" his mother asked as she finally pushed the last of the papers into her bag.

Alex, still watching his show as it beamed directly from his MeChip implant into his eyes, ears, and brain, paid her no attention.

"Alex? Alexander! Are you watching your show again? You know that's not allowed at mealtimes. MeChip, parental override. Switch off now!"

The image and sounds of Rock Shop Hero vanished and Alex found himself back in the kitchen and looking at one very irritated parent.

"How dare you watch something when I'm talking with you! Honestly, Alex, I've half a mind to take that MeChip of yours out," she said, arms folded across her chest.

"Take out my MeChip? That would be so weird," Alex replied, his fingers reaching for the back of his neck at the top of his spinal column where the MeChip implant lay beneath a small incision in his skin. His hand rubbed the spot for a moment, touching the small metal zip as if to reassure himself that the source of much of his enjoyment—from his favorite shows to his games and phone—was still there. "I mean, who doesn't have a MeChip these days?" he asked, not showing any contrition at all for ignoring the family rule about using the MeChip at mealtimes.

"No one, of course. You can be the first if you don't start listening. By the way, were you practicing your guitar again this morning?" she asked as the two of them rose and started towards the door.

"I guess so, yeah," Alex replied reluctantly.

"And what time were you up? 6:30?"

"Something like that. A little earlier, I guess."

"But that's great!" his mother said enthusiastically. "You know you can win this time. You have the talent. All it takes is hard work and some self-belief."

"Self-belief? After what happened last time? Anyway, I haven't even decided if I'll enter."

"Oh, you must, Alex! Just keep practicing and you'll be fine, I promise."

Alex didn't reply, merely raising both eyebrows as he tugged on the door, holding it open for her to go ahead.

Ten minutes later, a gleaming Ford Hydrocarb 3V swept silently through the gates of Lincoln High School and pulled into a parking space in front of a modern, opulent-looking building. The gull-winged doors swooshed upwards and Alex and his mother climbed out.

"Bye, Alex. See you in music class!" his mom shouted as Alex jogged away.

"Bye, Mom," Alex replied over his shoulder as he took the broad marble steps two at a time and strode quickly through the sparkling steel and glass entrance and into the spotless hallway.

Chapter Two
The Band

After depositing his beloved Laser Six-String guitar in his oversized locker, Alex made his way to the classroom and took his usual spot by the window, second row from the back. A minute later, two other boys walked in. One was tall and lanky with pale skin, freckles, straw-colored hair, and arms and legs so long and ungainly he looked like he had just emerged from a major growth spurt. He was smiling to himself, as if remembering a joke he'd been told. The other was shorter and looked like he was still waiting for his growth spurt to start. Unlike his lofty friend, this boy had a serious expression, dark skin, short curly hair, and powerful, muscular arms.

Tom and Sol, Alex's best friends, sat down on the two seats next to his.

"So?" Tom said, his white-blond eyebrows raised quizzically as he looked at Alex.

"So what?" Alex asked, avoiding the taller boy's gaze and instead looking towards the classroom door, where more teenagers were filing into the classroom in twos and threes.

"You know exactly what, Alex. Are we going to try again this year or what?

"Try at ...?" Alex replied, still playing dumb.

Tom was about to speak when the school PA crackled into life.

"Good morning, students! This is a final reminder that those wishing to compete in this year's Best Band contest must sign up at lunchtime today in the auditorium. Those who miss today's deadline will not be allowed to compete. No exceptions. Have a good day!"

There was silence for a few moments as both Tom and Sol stared at their friend.

"Oh, right, you mean try again at *that*!" Alex replied, finally.

"Duh! You really are such a smart Alec, Alex, and—"

"That joke never gets old. But you know I'm having trouble deciding," Alex said, finally looking his friend in the eyes.

"Well, you have about four hours to make up your mind before it's too late. Honestly, why are we practicing so hard if we're not going to compete?" Tom asked.

"Tom's got a point," Sol chimed in, sounding serious as he scratched his chin. "Look, I know it doesn't happen often. This may be the first time anything Tom said has made sense. But he's got a really good point now."

"Okay, okay! Look, I'll—" But Alex's reply was interrupted, for at that moment an elderly teacher entered the room and immediately started speaking in a commanding voice.

"Good morning, everyone. Now, we're going to start on something special today: George Orwell's classic novel, *1984*. It's set in a dystopian future that's the complete opposite of the world you're all lucky enough to inhabit. Pull it up on your MeChips, please."

"You'll what, Alex?" Tom said, ignoring the teacher.

"I'll ... I'll ... look, I haven't decided yet. I tell you what, I—"

"Mr. Alexander Franklin! I asked you to open Mr. Orwell's *1984*. Kindly cease your conversation with Mr. Hamilton and Mr. Tubman and access your MeChip's school page. You'll find you have access to this, and only this, so don't go trying to do anything else. In case you needed reminding, the school zone controls on your MeChip will tell me if you try to use it for any other purpose. Now, Orwell's *1984*, page one, please!"

Reluctantly, Alex and the rest of the class accessed the book *1984* with a simple mental instruction, which transmitted the request instantaneously from their brain's frontal lobes to their MeChips at the back of their necks. A copy of the book cover appeared in each student's vision, while the classroom receded behind it like a screensaver behind icons on an old computer.

"Alright, is everyone looking at page one of the book now?"

One or two nodded, but the others did not respond.

"Is that a 'yes'?" Ms. Monroe asked with an edge in her voice.

"Yes, Miss Monroe," more of the group replied.

"Honestly, you'd think I was asking you to do something difficult!" Ms. Monroe said, finally satisfied they had all done as instructed. "You know, in *my* day we didn't have the wonderful MeChip to bring books straight into our minds. You know what we had to use?"

The students exchanged looks and several rolled their eyes. Tom cupped a hand over his mouth so Ms. Monroe couldn't see his lips, then started to mouth silently what she was saying word-for-word, while Alex tried not to laugh and Sol just frowned. But Ms. Monroe would not have noticed anyways as she paced up and down, her well-worn speech now in full flight.

"No? Well, we had to carry *books*! Real life books! And they were heavy, too. We didn't have MeChips back then. Oh no! Honestly, you kids today don't know how lucky you are! And that's not all ..." she continued, pausing just for a moment to draw breath before launching further into her tirade.

A few hours later the bell rang for lunchtime and Alex, Tom and Sol burst out of a room along with the rest of the class.

"Was it just me or was that math challenge impossible?" Tom asked, scratching the back of his head.

"It was just you," Sol replied as the friends made their way down the corridor.

"Alright, alright. We all know you're a complete dexter who does equations in his sleep, Sol. How about you, Alex?"

"It was kinda hard for me, too."

"Can I tell you something that won't be hard?" Sol asked, his voice still serious.

"What?"

"Entering the Best Band competition," he replied as he led his friends around a corner and into the auditorium.

The first thing Alex saw as they entered the cavernous room was a hand-painted sign with the words "Best Band Contest: Sign Up Here!" It had been hung from the far wall above a fold-out table. A couple of dozen students had already gathered and were milling around. Alex could just make out his mother standing behind the table. As he watched, she placed a pen and a clipboard on the tabletop.

The three friends made their way towards the crowd where Alex suddenly stopped, hanging back. Tom turned to face him and looked down at his friend, a frown replacing his usual optimistic smile.

"Okay, Alex. Decision time. No more faffing about. I want to enter the competition. Sol wants to enter the competition. So ... are we going to do this or not?" he asked as Sol looked on, nodding his agreement.

Before Alex could reply, however, another student pushed past. He was as tall as Tom but his shoulders were broader, his physique already filled out and muscular. His blond hair was swept rakishly to the side, his eyes were marine blue, his smile confident and his teeth shiny and white. Behind him came three other strutting seniors, all wearing varsity jackets with the letters "LH Football" emblazoned on their chests.

"Make way, everyone. Clear the way. Iggy's here!" announced their leader as the crowd parted like the Red Sea and the gang made its way up to the table.

Alex looked on as Iggy picked up the pen, leaned over the clipboard, and casually wrote on the top sheet of paper.

"And it's done!" Iggy said, turning back to the crowd, his dazzling smile on full display. "Iggy and the Overlords are officially in the race. We're going to win it again. And the Nationals this time, too!"

Most of his audience started to applaud and half-a-dozen girls cheered and screamed their support for the handsome young man and his posse, who nodded and grinned at their fans before making their way triumphantly back through the press of students.

As Iggy emerged from the crowd he accidentally bumped into Alex, who staggered into Tom. Iggy looked Alex up-and-down, smirking as the other students watched.

"Franklin, I'm surprised to see you here after what happened last time. You're not really thinking of embarrassing yourself again, are you?" Iggy asked, raising his voice so the crowd could hear.

"I haven't decided yet," Alex replied quietly, looking at the ground.

"Well, if you do enter, can you repeat last year's performance? Funniest thing I've ever seen," he said, sniggering as most of the crowd joined in. "Humiliating for you, of course. But funny." He gave Alex one last, pitying look, shook his head, and walked out of the hall, his cronies in tow.

Iggy's words triggered something in Alex. Without warning, all the memories of last year's contest flashed irresistibly before his eyes.

He was back at the Best Band contest again, dressed in his rad costume and waiting with Sol and Tom to go onstage. He had never performed in front of such a big crowd, but he knew it would be fine. In that moment he had felt so confident, knowing their Rock Shop song was smeckin' cool and certain they'd be victorious. He hadn't cared that a Freshman band had never won before, because he wasn't just any *Freshman. He was Alex Franklin, uber guitarist. New as he was, everyone in the school already knew his name. Even that arrogant Junior, Iggy Elgar, was running*

scared. Sure, Sol was worried Alex hadn't practiced enough. But Sol was always worried about something. He'd been like that ever since they'd become friends in fourth grade. Alex knew they'd win on natural talent.

Of course, he had been wrong. In his mind's eye, he could see himself strutting onstage on that fateful night, ready to perform. There was Tom, kicking off the song on his drums, with Sol adding the bass. Now it was Alex's turn to come in on guitar after eight full beats.

And that was when it happened. Staring out into the vast crowd under the harsh glare of the stage lights, Alex's mind had gone completely blank. It was as if he'd forgotten not only the song, but how to play guitar at all. He could not for the life of him remember a single chord.

Still trapped in this awful memory, Alex pictured himself standing on stage, frozen in fear and missing his musical entrance as the guitar pick fell from his fingers. Tom and Sol were playing another eight beats, giving him a chance to recover. Again, nothing. They were trying a third time to play him in, but by now he was utterly paralyzed. As his mind replayed the scene in every dreadful detail, he recalled dimly thinking Sol had been right. He had been over-confident. He should have rehearsed more. Instead, he was standing stock still on the stage, unable to move a muscle as the muttering and mocking laughter began to ripple through the audience.

With a jolt, Alex came out of his daydream and looked around him. He wondered how long he'd been lost in thought. Thirty seconds? A minute? More?

Sol and Tom were watching him anxiously but the small crowd that had been in the auditorium earlier appeared to have lost interest after Alex's run-in with Iggy. Most had left the hall already, although Alex hadn't noticed them go. A handful of teenagers remained near the sign-up table; it looked like one was chatting with Alex's mom.

Alex ran his hand through his hair, trying to pull himself together. Part of his brain was still stuck in the past, though. He had never felt quite the same since that night. His mojo was gone, his faith in his musical abilities shot to pieces. His reputation, he knew, had been destroyed. He was a laughing stock: the kid who'd humiliated himself in front of the entire school; that big-headed Freshman whose arrogance exceeded his talent and had got what he deserved.

And here he was again, making a dexter of himself as he stood frozen and speechless in the hall. He took several deep breaths to calm himself, waiting until his heart rate slowed before finally turning towards his worried friends.

He was pretty sure what he needed to do. There was no way he could enter the Best Band contest again, he thought, his head still buzzing. Iggy was right; Alex would only humiliate himself. He could *not* could go through that again.

He was about to tell Tom and Sol his decision when someone tapped his shoulder. He turned around ... and felt his heart start to race once more.

"So *are* you going to enter the contest, Alex?" asked the girl as she stared at him searchingly.

Chapter Three

The Girl

The girl smiled, her chocolate-brown eyes level with his. Alex held her gaze for only a moment before looking away.

"Oh, hi Abby. I'm not sure. Last year didn't go so well, you know."

"I remember. But that was a long time ago. Things change. People change," she said, her head tilted a little to one side as she eyed him appraisingly.

"So, you think we *should* try again?" Alex asked uncertainly, trying not to look too hard into those wonderful eyes or to stare at her lustrous brown hair, which fell in light curls down to her shoulders.

"Of course you should enter! I heard you rehearsing over lunchtime the other week and you sounded great. I mean, really great! You should show everyone your skills."

"Really?"

"Really! *And* make Iggy eat his words!" she added, smiling.

"Oh, right. Well, yeah. That's ... that's what I was thinking, too."

"Great! Well, go on then," she said, nodding in the direction of the table where the sign-up sheet lay waiting.

Feeling a little self-conscious, Alex stepped forward. His mother smiled at him gently as he approached. Slowly, almost mechanically, as if someone else was directing his body, he picked up the pen, leaned over the clipboard and, trying to keep his hand steady, wrote *Xander and the Plan A's*. After last year's fiasco Alex had invented a stage name—Xander—for himself, in the hope it would make him more confident on stage and less like, well, himself. So far, it hadn't worked. After writing his entry, Alex scanned the list to see who else had entered. Above his name he saw *Iggy and the Overlords*. There was also *Saratoga Redux*, an all-girl band that had run Iggy a close second last year and whose bass player, Harriet, was widely regarded as one of the best musicians in the school. Five other bands were also on the list.

As he put the clipboard back down on the table, Abby clapped and whooped a solitary cheer, while the handful of people still in the room looked on and either chuckled or whispered to their neighbors. Smiling at him one last time, Abby turned and walked away, waving over her shoulder as Alex rejoined Tom and Sol.

"Well, we're in it now," Sol said. "And all because of a girl."

"Seems like a good reason to me. She is smeckin' tidy!" Tom answered, craning his neck to catch sight of Abby as she disappeared through the doorway.

"Hey!" Alex said, glaring at his friend in exasperation. "Dude, I told you. Don't check out Abby. Anyone else ... or in your case, everyone else! But not her. Okay?"

"Sorry, Alex. I didn't mean to check out the cute girlfriend you *don't* have. I guess I'll just leave that to the rest of the school!"

"Whatever," Alex muttered as they left the hall.

The three friends were on their way to the cafeteria and sauntering down another squeaky-clean corridor when a noise from a nearby classroom stopped them in their tracks. A guitar chord sounded, powerful and urgent, followed a moment later by the lower, insistent thrumming of the bass and, four beats later, the crashing of the drums. Four more bars of music followed, strong and strident. Alex could just make out, through a narrow window in the door, his nemesis and tormentor Iggy as the young man stood, feet wide apart and guitar slung across his torso, a microphone close to his lips. A moment later, Iggy opened his mouth and began to sing, his voice cutting above the music, his tone commanding, arrogant and, Alex had to admit, almost majestic:

"I can fly,
I can soar,
I can reign,
Over all.
Just so high,
I take wing,
Looking down,
I will win.
I'll succeed,
And why not?
Don't you know
That I've got,
The will to win again!"

Alex stood stock still, mesmerized as he listened to Iggy and his cronies rehearsing on the other side of the classroom door. With an effort he finally shook himself free of the spell and slunk away, heading down the corridor with Tom and Sol in tow as they retreated from the song, feeling relieved Iggy hadn't spotted them eavesdropping.

No one spoke as they entered the cafeteria, joined the line, grabbed trays and picked out their food. It was only after they sat down at an empty table that Tom finally broke the silence.

"He is good, though, isn't he?" he said, as if reading Alex's mind. "Arrogant, but smeckin' good."

"So are we!" Alex replied defensively.

"Of course we are." Tom agreed. "Just so long as—"

"So long as what? I don't mess up again?"

"No! That's not what I meant. Not exactly ..." Tom replied, his pale cheeks turning red.

"Yes, it is," Sol interrupted in his calm, baritone voice. "Because you, Tom, are a total dexter, with the sensitivity and tact of a bull elephant. But Alex won't mess up this time. Right, Alex?" Sol said, looking seriously at his friend.

"That's right, Sol," Alex agreed half-heartedly as he speared a potato on the end of his fork and wondered if he had convinced anyone, least of all himself.

A few hours later, the home bell rang and teenagers began flocking out of the school entrance and into the warm, welcoming sunshine. Some made their way quickly to the waiting school bus as it glimmered and shone in the light, while others left on foot or jumped into a waiting parent's hydrocar. A lucky few headed to the parking lot where their own vehicles could be found.

By the time Alex, Sol, and Tom emerged from the building and started slowly down the stairs, the crowd had already thinned. The three of them were talking—or more, accurately, arguing—about music, as usual. In fact, Alex was so immersed in the conversation he didn't notice Abby until she stepped directly in front of him. Alex looked up in surprise, saw who it was, and felt his stomach perform what felt like a double somersault.

"Hi Alex!" Abby said breezily, smiling at him.

"Hay Ibby. Uh, I mean, hi Abby," Alex replied as his stomach continued its acrobatics routine and his neck and cheeks began to feel alarmingly hot.

"I'm glad you signed up for the Best Band contest," she said.

"Oh, that. Yeah, me too," Alex mumbled in a tone he knew would not have convinced anyone.

"Anyhoo, what are you doing now?" Abby enquired.

Alex didn't respond for a moment. He was alarmed to discover his brain had disconnected from his mouth. With a supreme effort, he forced his lips to move.

"Do you mean what am I doing *now*? At this moment?" he said eventually, his voice cracking slightly from the strain.

"Yeah. That's what I'm asking," she replied. "It is Friday, after all. Any plans?"

Alex risked a glance at her and noticed she was still smiling, her perfectly-straight teeth just visible between her full lips. Again, the connection between *his* mouth and brain seemed to be malfunctioning. With another effort he stammered out a response.

"I'm going to practice band. I mean band practice. That's what I'm going to do. At Sol's. With Sol. And Tom. And, um, me."

"Oh. Okay. Well how about later? You wanna hang out later?" she asked.

"Later? Yes. Yes, definitely later. Absolutely. Me hang out with you, you mean?" he replied as his stomach continued to perform increasingly daring acts of agility as if building up to its gymnastic finale. Meanwhile, his heart was now drumming out a rapid percussion, perhaps to help it out.

"Yes, Alex, hang out with *me*," she said, shaking her head just slightly as she bit her lower lip. "Listen, I'll meet you at eight outside your front gate, okay?"

"Okay. I mean yes, for sure. Do you mind? Coming round to my place, I mean?" Alex asked.

"Alex, you live next door. I think I can handle the walk. See you at eight. And don't be late!" she added as she turned on her heel and walked back towards her girlfriends Martha, Sally, and Sybil, who were standing by the school gates and giggling as they observed the proceedings from a few paces away.

Alex watched them walk off, Abby now in the middle of the gang as they laughed and talked their way out of school and down the street. Sally and Sybil cast glances back in Alex's direction, although Abby herself did not turn back even once.

Slowly Alex's body started to return to normal: his stomach decided to end its aerobic routine; his heart rate dropped back from dangerous to normal speed; his brain re-engaged; and his cheeks and neck stopped superheating themselves. Now he merely felt dazed and distant, as if the whole scene had happened to someone else. Did that really just take place, he wondered?

Finally, a voice broke into his reverie.

"Smooth, Alex. Real smooth," said Tom, his voice dripping with sarcasm.

"You really do need to work on your chat-up lines, Alex. Seriously," Sol agreed.

"Okay, fair point. But ... she still asked me out, right? I mean, this is a date, isn't it?" he asked, unsure whether to trust his own senses.

"Yeah, it's a date, Alex. With your neighbor," Sol assured him, clapping him on the back and smiling for once.

"Your smeckin' cute neighbor!" Tom added. "Nice one, Alex! I'm officially jealous. Really. Abby is seriously tidy. Nice smile, pretty face, and a gorgeoulicious piece of—"

"Dude, cut it out! I told you, you can check out anyone but Abby, okay?"

"Okay, okay! Well, what about her friend Sybil, then? The redhead. She's not too shabby, either. Rather tidy, in fact. Alex, what's your policy on double dates?"

"I'm against them," Alex replied, unable to stop himself smiling as they walked through the gates of Lincoln High School and out onto the sidewalk.

The moment they set foot past the school gates, Alex heard a familiar voice inside his ear, courtesy of his MeChip:

School controls ended. Independent mode now on.

At the same time, a small yellow smiley face icon appeared in the corner of his vision, confirming he had full control of his MeChip once more.

Usually, Alex would have immediately pulled up a song to listen to while he walked. Not today. Today, he didn't want or need his MeChip. Today, all he wanted to do was talk with his friends about what had just happened in *real life*, to relive the moment when Abby Adams—*the* Abby Adams—had asked *him* out.

Twenty minutes later the three friends turned down Sol's street, still chatting about what had happened. Like Alex, Sol lived in a nice area. Poplar trees and broad sidewalks flanked the wide, well-maintained avenue. Retro-looking street lamps set at regular intervals, freshly-painted picket fences, and old-fashioned but beautifully-maintained colonial-style houses provided a pleasant contrast with the ultramodern, shiny hydrocars parked in almost every driveway.

Only a single discordant note would have struck an observer to this comfortable scene. As the friends opened Sol's gate, entered the garden path and made their way to their rehearsal space in the garage, a large, black hydrocar pulled around the corner, slowed, then parked about 50 yards away. The boys didn't notice it as they unpacked their gear, still talking animatedly about girls and music.

Whoever was inside was hidden behind tinted windows that were almost as dark as the paintwork. More curiously still, the vehicle had no license plates. It had a sinister aspect as it remained there, shadowed by a tree, its brooding presence in peculiar contrast to the otherwise cheery and sunny suburban scene. After a few minutes, as if sensing it didn't belong, the car engine growled to life once more and the vehicle pulled out from the curb and accelerated away, taking its shadowy malevolence with it.

Chapter Four
The Date

"Hold on a millisec, guys. *MeChip*, close the garage door!" Sol said. It responded almost instantaneously, closing completely as it shut them off from the street and the outside world.

"Shall we?" Sol said.

The others nodded.

"Alright then. One, two, three, four," Tom intoned as he started on drums, laying down a strong beat. Sol joined in next, his bass guitar adding a deep layer to the rhythm section for eight full bars before Alex strummed his guitar and, last but not least, brought his vocals into the mix.

They'd come up with the song as a joke. A fast-paced, Rock Shop number, it was Alex who'd penned the lyrics while Sol and Tom worked on the music. The song, *Iggy's Going Down*, would never be performed in public. They wouldn't dare. But it had made them laugh and was now firmly established as their "warm up" song at rehearsals. Alex relished the words as he sang, barely able to suppress a smile:

"Who loves himself more than anything?
Who'd date himself if he could?
While smooching his mirror ten times a day,
Oh Iggy, you know you would.
Whose hair shines like it's made of gold?
Who washes it five times a day?
Who's an arrogant bully who has no brain?
Oh Iggy, can you guess what they say?

Who thinks they're so special they'll win the prize?
Do you know that we'll beat you this time?
Cause we'll fight, we won't stop 'till we've got this down,
And we'll strip you of the Best Band Crown,
Yeah, we'll strip you of the Best Band Crown.

The three of them grinned as the song ended and Alex found himself praying their hopes and dreams would come true. It would feel so good to take Iggy down a peg or two.

"Okay guys, nice warm up. Now let's work on the numbers that are still in the running for when we perform at the Best Band contest," Sol said, getting down to business.

The band practiced hard for several hours, stopping only for a quick dinner. They had written three songs they agreed might be a good fit for the contest, but it wasn't clear which one was their best. All three needed practice, practice and more practice.

It was dark outside when Alex suddenly stopped singing, a frown on his face.

"Oh, smeck, it's nearly eight! I have to go or I'll be late. Thank your mom for dinner will you, Sol?" Alex asked as he placed his guitar carefully in its case.

"Will do. You know your MeChip has an alarm in it, right?" Sol said as he opened the garage door.

"Yeah, yeah. See you this weekend, alright?" he said as he started jogging down the street.

"You sure will. We want to hear everything that happens with Abby, got it? Everything!" Tom shouted after him as Alex rounded the end of the avenue and disappeared from view.

By the time Alex skidded around the corner of his street a quarter of an hour later, he was gasping for breath. He slowed a little as he approached his house, stopping a few yards away from Abby, who was leaning against his gate. Silently, he checked his MeChip for the time. It was 8:02.

"You're late," Abby said.

"Sorry, Abby. Lost track of time," Alex replied, trying to slow his breathing.

"You know your MeChip has an alarm in it, right?"

"Yeah. Sorry."

"No worries. How was practice?" she asked, sounding genuinely interested.

"Good. Pretty good. We still have a ways to go before we can compete with *Iggy and the Overlords*, though."

"You know, Alex, I think you're a lot better than you realize. I told you, I heard you rehearsing the other week and you guys are good—*way* better than I remember. You'll give Iggy a run for his money this time."

"Thanks, Abby," Alex said, remembering his mother's injunction to express appreciation for a compliment even if he privately didn't think he deserved it. "I sure hope we can."

"You just need to believe in yourself."

"I'll try," Alex promised.

"Anyhoo, changing subjects, do you remember the old tree house?

"What?"

"The tree house. You know, the one in my back garden we used to play in as kids?" she asked, a curious expression on her face.

"Um ... yeah. I guess," Alex replied feeling nonplussed at why she'd suddenly turned the conversation in such a seemingly random direction.

"Want to check it out?"

"Check out your old tree house?" Alex repeated, unsure he'd heard her correctly.

"Yeah. My old tree house. Come on, let's go look at it again. For old time's sake," she said, still wearing a wry smile and an expression Alex couldn't quite figure out.

"Um, yeah. Sure. Why not?" he shrugged.

"Good. Come on then."

Abby walked ahead of him up the street, Alex following close behind while trying not to stare too hard at her wonderful, flowing hair, her confident walk. Without warning, she stopped and turned around so quickly Alex almost bumped into her. Her face was now very close to his, that same secretive, knowing look in those deep brown eyes. They were the same height these days and Alex found himself starting to sweat again as she held his gaze. After a few moments, he looked away.

"Aren't we going to ... um ... open the gate?" he asked uncertainly, still not sure what was happening.

"No need," she said, as she placed one hand casually on the fence and vaulted expertly over in one graceful, athletic motion, then started to walk into the shadows of the garden towards the large oak tree behind the house.

Alex tried to follow, almost stumbling and falling flat on his face as he clambered over the fence in what he knew was a far more ungainly attempt than Abby's. Luckily for him she didn't look back as he finally got over the obstacle and began trotting after her into the darkness.

He caught up with her at the bottom of the wooden ladder, which led up into the tree above.

"Come on," she instructed, again leading the way as she climbed lithely upwards.

"Um, what about my guitar and pack?" he whispered.

"Leave them by the ladder. There's not much room up here," her voice came from above.

After placing the case and his school bag against the tree trunk, Alex began to follow Abby up the ladder. A memory came back to him as he climbed and he began to count, knowing somehow that there would be fifteen rungs in all. When was he last here, he wondered to himself? Five years ago, perhaps? More?

He reached the fourteenth step and reached up, knowing the platform—or floor—of the treehouse should be there, slightly to the right. But his memory had betrayed him, for his hand met empty space.

For a millisec he thought he would fall, imagining himself crashing through the lower branches to smash against the ground below. Then a hand caught his and steadied him, pulling him up and to the left where his fingers found the safety of wooden planks. With Abby's help, he hauled himself up.

"Thanks," he gasped as he drew himself into the little wooden structure that sat eighteen feet above the ground.

The tree house was smaller than he remembered and there was not much room for the two of them to sit as their legs dangled over the side of the platform on the one side without walls. As he breathed in, he caught Abby's scent, an alluring, strangely intoxicating combination of ... what? Flowers and peppermint, perhaps? He wondered if she was wearing perfume.

Neither of them spoke as they looked out onto the garden and the street. Alex's eyes began to adjust to the darkness and his other senses felt strangely heightened. Below them, he detected a black cat as it slunk through the neighbor's garden on some hidden business of its own. His ears picked up the rustle of the leaves around them as a light wind whispered by, while in the distance the hum of traffic was faintly audible from the highway that skirted the far side of town. He was suddenly aware of his own breathing. Finally, Abby spoke.

"So, what do you think?"

"It's nice," Alex said, not sure how to respond.

"I'm glad you like it. I still come up here sometimes, you know. I find it relaxing. It helps to get away from everything, to think, to disconnect," she said, a touch of melancholy in her voice.

"Um, yeah. I can see that," Alex agreed, wondering to himself what Abby might need to disconnect *from*. Wasn't her life pretty good?

"Do you remember how we used to play here?" Abby asked suddenly, the usual note of enthusiasm back in her voice.

"Of course!" Alex agreed. "We used to come up all the time. I have some really good memories of this place, now I think about it."

"Me too," Abby agreed.

There was a few seconds' silence before Abby spoke again.

"Anyway, back to the present. So, you know how you really want me to be your girlfriend?"

"Wait, what? Who told you? I mean, I never *said* that," Alex replied, feeling shocked and embarrassed, particularly since even though he'd never told her that, he *had* imagined it any number of times.

"Of course you didn't say it, Alex. But you do *want* that, don't you?"

Answers flashed through Alex's brain in quick succession. Should he deny it? Refuse to answer? Put the question back on her? He decided to stall ... to play for time while he tried to unscramble his brain.

"What makes you think I want that?"

"Alex, you've been avoiding me for months and acting like a complete dexter whenever I say hi—turning red, stumbling over words. It just isn't like you."

"Really?"

"Really, Alex. Look, we've been friends since we were five and then suddenly after nearly ten years you go all off-grid on me. At first I couldn't understand it: I thought maybe you just didn't like me anymore; that we'd grown apart or ... I don't know ... whatever. But then I paid a bit more attention to what you were doing, to your little glances at me in class and your sudden awkwardness and figured maybe, just maybe, your feelings had changed in a different way. So ... am I right?" she asked.

Alex snuck a sideways look at Abby trying to catch her expression, but her face was shadowed in darkness. How should he reply? Should he tell her the truth?

He was just screwing up his courage to speak when Abby spoke again.

"Hold on, my Dad's calling," she said, holding up her hand.

"Yes, Dad," she said, speaking curtly into her MeChip. "But can't I just have five more minutes? Okay, okay, I'll be right there. Bye."

"I have to go," she said, turning to Alex. "Can we pick this up again tomorrow? You're coming to my parents' barbecue, right?"

"What? Oh yeah. Sure," Alex replied.

Alex followed Abby down the wooden steps and grabbed his gear from the base of the tree as Abby walked quickly back to her house. She paused at the back door, turned, smiled briefly at him, then entered the house and closed the door behind her.

Alex stood there for several minutes in the darkness, trying to absorb what had just happened. It all had been so quick that he was still in shock. His heart was still racing as he realized how close he had been to telling Abby his secret—to telling Abby how much he liked her.

But what did *she* think of *him*? Had she asked up to the tree house to humiliate him? To warn him off? Tell him he didn't stand a chance? But then, why invite him around at all? She could easily have given him the cold shoulder at school rather than picking this quiet, private place. And why did she want to pick up the conversation again tomorrow? For a moment he allowed himself to think the unthinkable—that she liked him, too.

Alex walked to the side of her garden, climbed the fence, and made his way back to his house.

"Hey Mom, hey Dad! It's me. I'm home," he yelled as he opened the front door. "I had dinner at Sol's so just heading up to my room, okay?"

As he reached the bottom of the stairs his mom appeared from the living room.

"Hi Alex. How was your day? Good rehearsal?"

"Yeah, pretty good," he said.

"You look distracted. Everything okay?" she asked, noticing his frown.

"Yeah, I think so."

"Want to talk about it?"

"No, no, it's okay," he replied, quickly rearranging his features and wondering how he could ever tell his parents about what had just happened. "Everything's okay."

"You sure?"

"Yeah," he said, avoiding her eyes.

"Okay, Alex, keep your secret, then," she said, raising an eyebrow.

"Goodnight, Mom," he said as he made his way upstairs.

As soon as he had closed the door to his room, he dropped his bag, placed his guitar case carefully against the wall, and fell back onto his bed where he lay, hands behind his head, staring in an unfocused way at the ceiling.

"What just happened?" he asked himself out loud. "Did I just dream that?"

Before he could answer his own question, a text message popped up on Alex's retina:

ABBY: Goodnight, Alex. Thanks for tree housing with me. See you at my parents' BBQ tomorrow afternoon, okay?

Alex wrote back immediately: *Definitely! See you then.*

ABBY: Nite!

ALEX: Nite!

He was still lying on his bed trying to recall every detail of the evening and to figure out what it all meant when another message pinged him, this one from Tom.

TOM: How'd it go?

ALEX: Tell you when I see you.

TOM: What? No fair! Really? Can I just call you now?

ALEX: Not now. Let's catch up this weekend. Then we can talk in person, okay?

TOM: Fine. But I wanna hear everything that happened. No holding back. I'll ping you tomorrow.

ALEX: Sure. Nite, T.

TOM: Nite ... hotshot!

It was warm in his room and after a few minutes Alex got up and opened the window. As he did, the sound of music floated in. He looked out at Abby's house. Through an open curtain on the ground floor he could see a figure—Abby for sure—sitting at her Ultralux Synthi-Piano. Straining to hear the sound, he could just make it out as the notes carried softly on the night air.

She was performing an old Retro-Romwave tune. Alex vaguely remembered it from years ago. Normally he'd have dismissed it as too sickly sweet for his tastes, but the way she played made him reconsider. She really is good, he thought to himself as he heard the wistfulness and sentimentality she conjured with her fingers. He wondered for a moment why she hadn't entered the Best Band contest herself. She definitely had the chops for it. Almost without thinking, he took his guitar out of its case and began strumming quietly to himself, picking out a gentle accompaniment as the sound of her playing continued to carry through the open window, the simple act of playing sending a comforting, warm glow through his body.

Finally, her performance ended and he saw her stand up and walk away from her instrument. A moment later the light went out from the downstairs room. She, too, was evidently heading to her bedroom.

A few minutes later, Alex had brushed his teeth and was back on his bed, lights out but still staring at the ceiling.

What a surprising world, he thought. Who'd have thought, when he woke up this morning, that he'd end up hanging out with Abby in her tree house? Or that she'd ask him to meet up with her again tomorrow? His heart began to beat a little faster at the thought of seeing her again.

It took him a long time to find sleep that night. But when he finally did, his lips bore just the faintest trace of a smile.

Chapter Five
Ketchup and Blood

Alex swallowed nervously as he pulled open the gate, holding it wide for his mom and dad to pass into the garden. He had woken late and spent Saturday morning practicing guitar and then—at his parents' insistence—doing his weekend chores: tidying his bedroom, washing and drying his clothes, vacuuming, clearing the dishes after breakfast and lunch.

Usually, Alex would have done his chores to the accompaniment of his MeChip. He would summon his favorite music—mostly Synthipop, Rock Shop, or the latest Thrashtech—helping the work fade into the background and the time fly by. Today, though, he was too excited to listen to anything. The prospect of seeing Abby again so soon after what had happened last night was just too distracting to think about anything else.

The Adams family's garden was already quite crowded as Alex and his parents walked up the path and along the side of the house. Alex saw Abby's father first. He was working the barbeque, as always, flipping burgers while talking with a couple of neighbors.

Alex scanned the crowd until he saw Abby. She emerged from the side door carrying more hot dogs and buns, which she placed on a fold-out, plastic table by her father. She was wearing biz-hippie jeans and a florachromal t-shirt with matching banglettes. Her dark hair hung in ringlets to her shoulders and Alex felt his heart skip as he saw her. She was so *uber* tidy, he thought. *Now for the moment of truth.*

Abby looked up at that precise moment, saw Alex gazing at her, smiled in return, and immediately headed towards him. Alex stood still, rubbing the palm of his right hand with the thumb of his left in anxious expectation. A moment later and Abby was in front of him, thumbs hooked in her hip-belt, a smile playing across her full lips.

"Hi Abby. How are you?" Alex asked, feeling self-conscious and very aware of his pounding heart.

"Pretty good, thanks. C'mon, let's find somewhere quiet we can talk. Perhaps we can check out the treehouse again?" she said, arching an eyebrow as she turned on her heal and began leading him towards the back garden.

They were passing the barbecue when it happened. Abby's father, who had been grilling the food and chatting away with friends, began coughing. At first, he tried to shrug it off with a smile and a muttered apology. But it didn't stop, and after a few seconds he put a hand over his mouth and turned his body away from his friends as he tried to recover his composure.

The coughing continued. Alex watched in growing concern as the man's convulsions carried on with ever-greater violence. Unable to stop, he bent forward, hacking away for half-a-minute or more, both hands now covering his mouth. A neighbor stepped forward and tried to help while the other guests around the garden began to notice and look on with concern.

Finally, the fit abated and Abby's father slowly straightened up, gazed down at his palms, then looked at his friends and neighbors in shock.

Blood.

Blood coated his hands, drip-drip-dripping between his fingers and onto the freshly-cut grass below.

Blood drenched his apron, obscuring the "World's Best Dad!" declaration etched in bold blue letters under the tide of red.

Blood stained his shoes, his pants, his socks. It coated his mouth with a garish crimson, like the face of a toddler who has smeared themselves with their mother's lipstick.

Alex saw the man's look of incomprehension, witnessed the shock and fear among his neighbors as they crowded around to help.

And then ... nothing.

There was a moment of utter silence when nobody moved, nobody spoke. Quite suddenly, as if someone had flicked a switch, everyone simply turned away, went back to their conversations, to their beers and burgers.

Even Abby's father, after a slight pause, wiped his hands on his apron and returned to the barbecue, his attention now back on the hot dogs and buns.

After a few more seconds he coughed again, spitting up more blood, although less now; only a few flecks.

This time no one paid him any attention at all. Even Abby's father seemed barely to notice, wiping the blood from the corner of his mouth distractedly as he concentrated on not burning the meat and veggie dogs that were now sizzling and spitting on the grill.

The whole time Alex had been frozen to the spot, too surprised to move, let alone help. Now he felt released. He rushed towards the man and touched his arm.

"Mr. Adams, are you okay?"

"Oh, hi Alex. I didn't see you arrive. Me? Yes, of course. I'm fine. Why do you ask?" he enquired, looking slightly confused.

"You were just coughing a lot and there's ... well, there's blood on your apron and on your hands."

"Blood?" Mr. Adams replied. "No, Alex. This is ketchup. I just see a bit of ketchup. Plain and simple."

"Dad? Alex? What's going on? Is everything okay?" Abby asked as she followed Alex, stepping towards them.

"Yes, I think so," replied Mr. Adams. "That is, Alex seems to think I'm not well. He thinks this ketchup's actually *blood*," he said, looking quizzically at them both.

"But Mr. Adams, it *is* blood," Alex said, now just as confused as Abby's dad. "You were just coughing and blood came up. A lot of blood. Didn't it, Abby?" he said, turning to her.

"Yes," Abby replied, then paused. Slowly, almost mechanically, she ran a hand through her hair as her eyes clouded with uncertainty. Finally, she seemed to pull herself together:

"I mean, no. Alex, no one was coughing. This is ketchup. I just see a bit of ketchup. Plain and simple," she said, slowly and clearly.

Before Alex could reply, Mr. Adams turned to Alex's parents, who were standing nearby.

"Ben, Liz, your son was saying he sees blood on my apron. I'm trying to figure out if he's pranking me?"

"Well, it's a pretty morbid prank, Alex," his dad said, looking at him curiously as he glanced at Mr. Adams' apron. "This is ketchup. I just see a bit of ketchup. Plain and simple."

"What are you talking about, Dad?" Alex said in surprise. "Mom, help me out here ... please!" he said, looking to her for support.

For a moment she, too, looked perplexed. Then her face cleared.

"Alex, this is ketchup. I just see a bit of ketchup. Plain and simple."

Alex took a step back from them all, his mind reeling. What was going on? Were they all mad? Was he?

"Are you okay, son? You don't look well," his dad asked, looking concerned.

"But I saw ... you *all* saw ... I have to go," Alex declared as he turned and fled back up the garden path.

He had no idea what was going on. He only knew he needed to get away from them all right now, to get away from the blood, to clear his head and—

Slam!

He had not been looking where he was going. As he reached the gate, he had turned back and saw Abby staring at him, her eyes narrowed with some indecipherable emotion. And at that exact moment he had run into someone. That *someone* was evidently a lot bigger than him, for the collision had caused him to fall backwards onto the grass.

He looked up, shaking his head slowly to clear his bewildered brain.

Iggy.

The muscular teenager towered over him, a leering grin plastered across his face.

"Watch where you're going, dexter!" he hissed as he stepped over his fallen rival and strode confidently down the path towards the party.

Alex stood up and dusted himself off, then moved aside as a tall, attractive, middle-aged woman passed him without a second glance. Belatedly, Alex recognized her as Iggy's mother.

Resisting the urge to look back again, Alex stumbled through the open gate and ran towards his own house. In moments he was at the front door and fumbling for his keys. His hands were shaking so much it took him several seconds to unlock it, but finally he was inside. He lurched to the bathroom just in time as a wave of nausea overwhelmed him.

The room was long and windowless. The lights were dimmed, casting only a faint glow upon the dozens of holo-screens set at regular intervals along each wall. In front of each monitor sat a uniformed figure, their faces hidden in shadow. Occasionally one of them would reach up and touch the display with an outstretched finger and manipulate the image, or else speak softly into an earpiece.

One of the figures leaned forward, peering more closely at a moving image. It was a grainy picture of the Adams family's house and garden, looking down from above the road; the sort of view you might get from the top of a streetlamp or tree. The watcher saw Alex as he ran from the scene, was floored by Iggy, got up, and stumbled home. Using his thumb and forefinger to magnify the view, the figure focused it on Abby's father and his scarlet-stained smock. Next, he rotated the image to catch Alex's terrified face as he unlocked his door, flung it open, and slammed it behind him. For several seconds, the figure did not move or speak as the camera—or whatever was filming the scene—continued to show Alex's front door, now firmly shut. Finally, he spoke quietly but urgently into his earpiece:

"Controller, this is F451/1984. There's something you *need* to see."

Chapter Six
The Night Visitors

Alex knelt on the bathroom floor. His mouth tasted sour and bitter from throwing up and the room smelled like a trash can that hadn't been emptied in a month. After several minutes, the wave of nausea passed. He stood up and took three long breaths, steadying himself against the wall. Leaning forward, he flushed the toilet and turned towards the sink, located the mouthwash and gargled thoroughly. That done, he left the room and walked slowly and unsteadily up the stairs. He opened his bedroom door, shut it behind him and stepped towards his window, pulling the half-closed curtains apart. He rubbed his eyes with his knuckles to clear his vision and looked out, afraid at what he might see.

Normal. It was all completely normal. The barbecue was still going on and a couple of dozen people remained in the Adams' garden, talking and laughing, eating and drinking. Mr. Adams continued to operate the barbecue, chatting with his elderly neighbor from across the street while he fixed her a veggie dog. Alex could see the red stain on his apron. Was it blood? Or just ketchup? From this distance, he couldn't be sure. The only difference he could detect was that the air seemed strangely hazy. What was it? Smoke from the barbecue? Fog? That seemed unlikely.

His eyes wandered and he saw his parents chatting with Mr. Jay from the large house on the corner. But where was Abby? He scanned the crowd until he finally caught sight of her by the oak tree. She looked deep in conversation.

With Iggy.

Alex felt his mind whirl again with ... what? Anger? Jealousy? Why was she speaking to *him*, of all people?

But did it matter after what he'd just seen? Did anything matter after he had witnessed someone spew up so much blood; blood only *he* had seen?

Was it blood? No one else seemed to think so. They had all said it was ketchup.

But Abby had seen it too, at least for a second. Hadn't she? And what about the others? Was his memory deceiving him, or had everyone else looked shocked for a millisec, too? Before they had all turned away and seemingly forgotten about it, of course.

Surely that made no sense? Had he just been imagining things? Hallucinating, perhaps?

Another jarring thought struck him; could he be going crazy? Seeing things no one else could see? Is this what madness felt like?

He tried to remember if he'd ever experienced anything like it before. He *did* recall feeling really depressed after last year's Best Band contest. He had felt so utterly, completely humiliated. But even in his darkest moments he hadn't seen things that weren't there. So why would it be happening now, especially when he was no longer depressed and when things seemed to be going so much better?

He tried again to calm himself and began to take more deep breaths.

In-two-three-four; Out-two-three-four.

And again.

And again.

Feeling a little less panicked, he sat down on his bed and, almost without thinking, reached for his guitar.

His fingers caressed the laser strings, found a major chord—a happy, relaxing chord— and strummed. Music could always soothe him.

He sat there letting his subconscious mind guide his fingers, which moved seemingly of their own free will until they found their beautiful escape. His friend Tom pinged him on his MeChip twice, but he ignored it and continued on his guitar, finding solace and peace in his playing.

It was early evening when he heard the outside door slam, followed by footsteps in the hall and on the stairs. There was a knock on his door and his mom entered.

"Alex, are you okay?"

"Yeah. I think so. That is, I thought I saw ... I could have sworn I saw Abby's dad—"

"Mr. Adams is fine, Alex. But I'm worried about you. It's not like you to behave like that. Were you pranking him?"

"No. I swear!" he insisted, seeing her eyebrows rise in disbelief.

"Perhaps you were imagining it, then?"

"I guess," he said, shrugging.

"Listen, Alex, perhaps you should get an early night? After all, you've had some long days lately, what with all your band practices and so on. What you need is a good night's sleep. I'll tell you what; why don't I rustle you up some pizza before you turn in."

"Okay, Mom, sounds good," he replied quietly. His mother stared at him for a few moments before heading downstairs. This time, she left Alex's door wide open.

Alex opened his eyes. It was dark in his room and there was no sign of daylight through the curtains. Checking his MeChip, he saw it was exactly 2 a.m. What had woken him? Usually, he was such a sound sleeper his mom and dad had trouble waking him in the morning.

He lay there listening, his brain groggy and slow. For several seconds there was nothing, not a noise of any kind to puncture the silence, not even a light breeze ruffling the leaves. Then a metallic, clicking sound came from the street outside. Not noisy enough to rouse the neighborhood, but loud enough to jerk him into full wakefulness. He pushed aside the covers from his bed, sat up, got unsteadily to his feet and tottered towards the window where he cautiously pulled back one of the curtains.

At first, he could see almost nothing. It was a dark night and the new moon cast barely a glow, while the nearest streetlamps were almost fifty yards away. Then a flicker of movement caught his eye. Dark shapes had emerged from the shadowy street. Behind them, on the near side of the road, he could just make out the dim outline of a large SUV parked half hidden behind one of the trees lining the sidewalk.

The figures may have been hard to distinguish, but it was clear where they were going. One of them opened the gate to the Adams family's property and led the group purposefully towards the front door. They exchanged no words and walked in silence, as if not wishing to draw attention to their alien presence in the street. Alex watched them reach the house and stop as if waiting for something to happen.

Perfectly on cue the door opened, sending a shaft of light streaking up the garden path. Alex was shocked to see Mrs. Adams. She seemed subdued and passive, her head lowered, her hands dropping slowly down to her sides once she had opened the door.

Now the light was on her visitors, Alex could see they wore dark suits, long trench coats, and wide-brimmed, black hats. There were five in all. Probably men, Alex guessed, although he could not be sure since almost every inch of them was covered up. One of them—the tallest—was holding a long, black bag.

They filed into the house one-by-one, speaking neither to each other nor to Mrs. Adams, who stepped aside to admit them, her head still lowered. As soon as the last one entered, Mrs. Adams mechanically closed the door, plunging the garden into darkness once more.

Alex stood breathlessly, waiting for something to happen. He saw a light turn on in another downstairs room, then a second one go on upstairs. Shadows moved within but the curtains remained closed. A minute passed, then another and another. Should he do something? Call the Regs, perhaps? But what would he tell them? That a neighbor had, of her own free will, let some strangers in dark clothes into her house? He'd sound crazy.

He had almost made up his mind to wake his parents when the Adams' front door reopened. Once more, Mrs. Adams was visible as she pulled on the handle and sluggishly stepped aside.

Four of the figures re-emerged. They carried what appeared to be a stretcher. Something was on it covered in a blanket. Whatever it was must have been heavy, for the four figures toiled with its weight as they shuffled back down the garden path towards their vehicle.

One of the strangers lost their footing on a loose paving stone and lurched forward, almost tripping. The stretcher jerked to one side and although they managed to hold on and regain their balance, one edge of the blanket slipped off. Only then did Alex see for the first time what was concealed beneath.

Mr. Adams.

His eyes were closed, his face ghostly pale in the slender stream of light slipping from the house. A thin line of dried blood trailed from his blue lips, snaking around his jaw and beneath his neck.

Alex looked on in horror at the sickening scene, knowing it could only mean one thing.

Mr. Adams was dead.

Chapter Seven
Mistaken Identity

Alex cried out. He couldn't help it; what he had seen was too terrifying to stay silent.

His cry was not loud, surely not audible through his closed window. Yet whether it was his utterance or something else that alerted them, one of the dark figures turned and looked up in Alex's direction, its face lifted towards him.

Panicked, Alex ducked down and hid beneath the window frame. He was still cowering on the floor—concealed and too frightened to risk another glance outside—when he heard car doors closing, a motor come to life, and the squeal of tires as a vehicle accelerated away.

Cautiously, he lifted his head and looked out of the window.

Nothing. There was nothing there. No car. No strangers. Even Mrs. Adams had disappeared from view, her front door closed and the house plunged once more into darkness.

It was like none of it had ever happened.

Alex sat there for a long time, knees raised up close to his face, fingers interlaced over the back of his head, his body trembling slightly as he rocked rhythmically backwards and forwards.

He was on the verge of waking his parents several times, of bursting into their room and telling them exactly what he'd seen. Yet every time something held him back. What was it? Was he worried they would not believe him, would chastise him for pranking them or tell him he'd been dreaming? Or was he afraid he'd imagined it all and that his parents would decide he was losing his mind?

His MeChip showed it was 3:07 a.m. when he finally raised himself off the floor and crawled back into bed, determined to get some rest if he could.

Yet when he finally succeeded it was an uneasy slumber filled with strange dreams and a constant foreboding that someone—or something—was behind him, creeping up on him and ready to strike a crushing blow at his back or head or neck; or else that he had started to cough up blood like the doomed, dead Mr. Adams.

It was 9:45 a.m. when Alex entered the kitchen the next morning, rubbing his eyes and feeling, if anything, more drained than when he'd gone to sleep.

"Are you okay son?" his dad asked as he looked up from the Sunday paper and his morning coffee. "You look exhausted."

"I'm not great, Dad. But listen, did either of you see or hear anything last night? Anything unusual?" he asked, looking searchingly at each of them in turn.

Alex's parents looked unsure for a moment. His father scratched his chin, as if in thought. Then they both dropped their gaze, shook their heads mechanically, and replied at the same time:

"No, son. Slept like a log. Just like a log."

That was weird, Alex thought as he looked at them both. I mean, what were the chances they'd say exactly the same thing at exactly the same time?

If it was unusual, though, his parents evidently hadn't noticed. His dad looked back down at his paper while his mom nodded at the stovetop.

"There's still some eggs and hash browns left if you want some," she said before turning back to her book and half-finished mint tea.

Frowning, Alex wandered over to the food, piled some on a plate and joined them at the kitchen table. The three of them sat in silence for several minutes. In spite of his fatigue and anxiety, he found himself wondering yet again why older people still insisted on reading hard copy books and newspapers? Then he pushed the thought aside. There were more important things to worry about right now and he knew it.

He was still trying to summon the courage to bring up last night's events again when his father laid aside his paper, stood up, and looked at him.

"Alex, can you help me take out the recycling, please?"

"Sure." Alex deposited his empty plate in the sink and followed his father into the garage.

A few moments later the two of them emerged holding heavy bags full of empty plastic containers, broken down cardboard boxes and old paper. They carried them to a large recycling bin that stood close to the street near the fence adjoining the Adams family's property.

They had just finished dumping the recycling into the bin and were about to turn back to the house when Alex heard Abby's voice. She had emerged from her house and was running towards him. He waited, his father just behind him, as Abby reached the fence and stood on the other side a few feet away, looking at him anxiously.

"Alex! I'm glad I saw you. How are you feeling? Is everything okay?"

"Not exactly. But I'm more concerned about you. I ... did you sleep well?" he asked.

There was a slight pause as she frowned and ran a hand through her hair before her face cleared and she answered.

"Oh yes. Slept like a log. Just like a log."

Alex looked at her uncertainly. Wasn't that what his parents had said? Was it another weird coincidence? But he couldn't worry about that now. Now he'd started, he had to keep going, to ask this all-important question.

"And your father? Is he ... okay?" he asked, dreading the answer.

"Of course," Abby answered breezily. "You can ask him yourself if you like. He's just over there."

She pointed to the far side of their front yard where a man was dumping garbage into an oversized bin, his back to them. Alex saw him, relief mingling with confusion. Had it all been a dream, then? His imagination playing tricks with him?

Before Alex could respond, Abby had called over.

"Dad! Can you come here for a millisec. Alex wants to ask you something."

The man turned around, smiled at Alex and began walking towards them. He was wearing faded blue jeans and a favorite t-shirt Alex had seen Abby's dad wear many times, usually on weekends. As he approached, he looked from Alex to his father in friendly recognition, a reassuring smile on his face.

Everything was just as it should be, Alex realized, except for one simple detail.

This man—the man Abby had just called "Dad"—was *not* her father.

Chapter Eight
Grounded

Alex gasped and took a step backwards.

"Alex, are you alright?" asked the man who wasn't Abby's dad. "You look like you've seen a ghost." He was smiling, but Alex could not return his friendly gaze.

"Who are you?" Alex asked, unable to take his eyes off this complete stranger.

"Who am I?" the man repeated, frowning. "Alex, are you pranking me again, like at the barbecue yesterday?"

"Alex, what's going on?" Abby cut in nervously. "You *know* this is my dad."

"You know it is *not*," he shot back, looking incredulously at Abby. "Look at him, Abby! I mean, yes, he's the same height and his hair isn't so different. But it's not him. For a start, this guy has blue eyes; your dad's were brown. And your father doesn't have a mole on his chin."

"Of course he does!" Abby said, her voice growing more agitated. "He's had it as long as I can remember. In any case, I think I should know what my own father looks like," she insisted.

"Then you know as well as I do it's not him," Alex replied, feeling his temper rising along with a growing sense of panic and confusion. "Abby, your father is *dead*. I saw it last night. Those people came and took him away on a stretcher."

"What are you talking about? How can you say something so horrible?" she answered, her voice cracking as his shocking words hit home.

Alex felt his father's restraining hand on his shoulder.

"That's enough, Alex. If this is some sort of prank then it's in pretty poor taste. Apologize to Mr. Adams and Abby right now."

"Apologize to this imposter?" Alex answered, looking with revulsion at the phony in front of him. "No way!"

"Then you are grounded, Alex. Get back in the house right now," his father ordered. His voice was quiet and seemingly calm, but Alex recognized the edge in it, that tone his father had whenever he wanted his son to know that he, Alex, was skating on thin ice.

Alex looked from one face to the next: Abby's reflecting incomprehension mixed with alarm and distress; his father's showing suppressed anger; and Mr. Adams—or whoever he really was—simply seeming confused. Mind racing, Alex turned away and stumbled back towards the house, slamming the door behind him. In his mind's eye he could already imagine his father offering an apology to Mr. Adams and Abby for his behavior. As if any of this was *his* fault!

Tearing down the hallway and taking the stairs three at a time, he was in his room in seconds. He closed the door and threw himself on his bed, breathing hard as his head span.

What was going on? He felt like his whole world had been turned upside down and inside out. Who was the stranger? And how could anyone think he was Abby's father? It was insane!

Before he could begin to unscramble his thoughts he heard the front door open and his parents' voices below. His father's was loud and he distinctly heard the words, "He's done it again!" Then his mother replied in a softer, calming tone that was harder to hear. Both voices lowered and Alex could not make out anything else.

The outcome was soon clear enough, however. A couple of minutes later there were footsteps on the stairs and Alex's mom entered his room, this time without knocking.

"Alex, your father just told me what happened with Mr. Adams. What is going on? Were you pranking them or something?"

"I'm not pranking anyone, Mom. That guy is not Abby's dad. He was coughing up blood yesterday and now he's—"

"He's what? Listen to me, Alex. I saw John Adams through the kitchen window less than five minutes ago and he looks perfectly fine to me. You owe him an apology. Honestly, I'm starting to worry about you. This isn't funny and it just isn't like you."

"You think I'm joking, Mom? Can't you see it's not the same guy? Your MeChip vizo-specs must be busted if you're too blind to see the difference! There's no way I'm going to apologize to some stranger who's impersonating our neighbor. In fact, I've a good mind to call the Regs—"

"Alright, Alex, that's quite enough. I have no idea why you think it's amusing to pretend someone we've known for years is a fraud. If you were trying to impress Abby with this farcical nonsense, you're very much mistaken. Your father said she seemed very upset."

"I'm not trying to impress Abby. I'm trying to *protect* her! Listen, there's some weirdo in her house posing as her dad and none of you seem to have noticed. Am I the only one who's not crazy here?" he shot back angrily.

"And that's your last word, is it?" his mother asked, arms crossed.

Alex felt so angry and frustrated he didn't trust himself to respond. His mother waited for a few moments but when he didn't reply, she spoke again.

"Very well. If you insist on keeping up this ridiculous charade there's no point continuing the discussion. You're grounded. Honestly, I don't know what you're playing at, but you can stay in your room until you apologize. And no using your MeChip to contact your friends or watch a show, either. Parental override—Level 5!" she ordered, shutting down his MeChip privileges instantly.

She stared at him searchingly for several seconds but Alex would not meet her gaze. Finally, she sighed and left the room, closing the door firmly behind her. Alex punched his pillow a dozen times in quick succession, unable to contain his exasperation and fury.

This was so unfair! Just what was wrong with them all that they couldn't see that man was a phony?

And that was the real question, wasn't it? Just what *was* wrong with them that they thought a complete stranger was Abby's dad? Something was badly off here. He needed to figure it out, and fast.

As always when he felt sad or angry or anxious, he reached for his guitar, trying to find clarity and solace in his music. He started with some gentle, open chords, letting his fingers find the keys automatically, as if on autopilot.

But even his playing was astray today. As his mind kept returning to the horrors of the past twenty-four hours, he unconsciously drifted into minor chords and jarring, dissonant directions, with D minor and B flat continually rearing their malicious heads and only making his mood worse. For once, music had let him down.

Giving up, he placed his guitar carefully back in its case, unwilling even in this angry state to harm his beloved instrument. His nerves were shredded and his thoughts utterly disordered. His hands were shaking as he lay down on his bed, pushed his face into his pillow, and wept.

Chapter Nine
Iggy's Girl

Alex rubbed his eyes as he entered the kitchen next morning. He had spent the previous day in his room, emerging just once for a dinner with his parents that had been memorable only for the lack of any conversation—of which there was usually plenty. He had slept fitfully that night, waking frequently from twisted and disturbed dreams where the worst moments of the past two days played on a torturous loop. In the morning, he had woken feeling worse than ever.

His father looked up from his newspaper but didn't speak as Alex sat down at the kitchen table. The awkward silence continued for several seconds as Alex helped himself to cornflakes and milk, ignoring his parents completely. Finally, his mother addressed him, her tone more frosty than usual.

"Good morning, Alex. Is there anything you'd like to say to us?"

"No," he replied sullenly.

"Are you sure?"

"Yes."

"Very well. On your head be it, then."

Alex was not sure how to reply to that so chose not to, instead resuming his eating. A minute later, his mother spoke again.

"I'm going to leave now, Alex. Would you like a lift?"

"No. I'll bus it."

"Alright. But remember, I want you back home straight after school."

"What about band practice?" he replied, alarmed.

"Grounded means grounded, Alex. No practice. In fact, no anything except school and home until you apologize. Understand?"

Alex angrily thrust his breakfast aside, shouldered his backpack and marched out of the house, ignoring his father's calls for him to take his dishes to the sink.

The sun was shining and the sky was an uninterrupted azure blue, but Alex barely registered the perfect weather as he stormed down the street and turned the corner, his thoughts clouded by everything that had happened. He arrived at the bus stop just as the vehicle pulled up, jumped on board, and scanned its occupants. Abby wasn't on it but Sol was sitting at the back alone. Alex made his way up the aisle and took the seat next to him.

"Why'd you go all off-grid on us this weekend?" Sol began as soon Alex sat down. "Tom was going Crazy-Clinton on me all weekend because you wouldn't reply to his texts. You probably have a million MeChip messages from him by now."

"Sorry, Sol. I got grounded. All MeChip privileges are gone. My mom's limited it to essential services only, so I can't even check messages."

"That's heavy, man. What happened?"

"I'm not sure where to start. It's all kinda weird. Can we talk about it later, Sol?"

"Fine with me, Alex, but it won't satisfy Tom. You know he hates secrets; and loves gossip! But if that's how you feel, let's talk about the Best Band contest instead. Are we still on for practice tonight?"

"No, I have to go straight home after school. We'll have to practice at lunch until I can persuade my mom to lift the ban."

"Seriously? Listen, we've got to make your mom change her mind. I'll talk to her, okay? She knows how important this is."

"Why not? She thinks you're the responsible one of the group, so it's worth a try," replied Alex thoughtfully. "But I'll book a room to rehearse in at lunchtime, too, just in case."

"Good idea, Alex. Honestly, we probably need to practice morning, noon, *and* night if we're going to stand a chance against Iggy. Time's running out and we haven't even agreed on our best song."

"I know, I know. We need to make a decision soon."

"Then let's run through our top three over lunch. I still like the slower Retro-Romwave number, but I know you and Tom like the more upbeat songs more."

"I just think we need something that'll get the crowd worked up. We know Iggy will throw down a Thrashtech or Rock Shop tune to wow them. We're going to have to beat him at his own game."

"I'm not sure. Oh, speak of the Devil, there's the man himself," Sol said as the bus pulled up in front of Lincoln High School.

"Where?" Alex asked.

"You missed him. He just walked through the gates."

The two of them disembarked as the bus disgorged students into the crowded street. Tom was waiting for them by the gates and the three of them followed a tide of teenagers working their way into the school yard and towards the gleaming doors.

"What the smeck happened to you this weekend?!" Tom began, but Sol cut him short.

"Save it, Tom. He's grounded but doesn't want to talk about it yet. Okay?" Sol said on Alex's behalf.

"What? No fair! Come on, spill the beans, Alex! What happened?" Tom begged.

"We were talking about what song to choose if we're to beat *Iggy and the Overlords*," Sol continued, ignoring Tom's objections.

"Oh, him. There he is with his girl," Tom said, nodding at the crowd in front of them. "Why do braggster no-goods like him always end up with the smeckin' tidy ones?" Tom muttered angrily.

Alex followed Tom's gaze and saw Iggy for the first time. He was a few paces ahead and slightly to one side. He was making out with a girl, seemingly oblivious to the crowd of fellow students, some of whom snickered or pointed at the amorous couple as they passed by.

Iggy's back was turned to Alex and at first he couldn't see who Iggy was kissing. He felt a bit surprised, since although Iggy never had a problem meeting girls Alex had heard that he'd broken up with his last girlfriend, Charlotte Riedesel, only the other week.

Alex had decided to ignore his rival and not even look at him, but as the three friends came alongside Iggy, Alex's curiosity got the better of him and he snuck a peak at the affectionate pair. It was then he saw Iggy's partner. Gasping in shock, Alex began to push his way towards them.

"No way. No smeckin' way!" he said as he forced his way through the crowd, unable to believe his eyes. A wave of uncontrollable fury overwhelmed Alex as he reached up and grabbed the taller boy's shoulder with his left hand, pulling him back with all his strength. Iggy took a step back and turned to face Alex, his eyebrows raised in surprise. He opened his mouth to speak but before a word could come out Alex had swung his right fist, catching Iggy a fierce blow in the cheek.

"Get your dirty, stinkin' hands off her!" Alex shouted, overcome with rage.

Alex's punch sent Iggy staggering backwards, but somehow the bigger boy stayed on his feet. He looked at Alex, rubbed his cheek slowly, looked down at his fingers, balled them into fists, then struck back with a swift left jab that caught Alex's ear, followed by a ferocious, hard right that caught him square in the mouth.

Alex was knocked backwards by the force of the blows and fell hard to the ground. Still, he felt no pain as the adrenaline surged through his body. Instantly, he was back on his feet and tried to launch himself at his taller enemy, but found firm hands holding him back. He turned to see Sol and Tom on either side, their fingers gripping his arms as they spoke to him urgently, trying to calm him down as he strained against them. But the words didn't sink in. He was still too shocked, too angry, for any self-restraint.

He looked from Iggy, who was now smirking cruelly at him, to the girl, who was staring open mouthed, a look of astonishment on her beautiful face.

"Alex, what are you doing?" she said quietly. The crowd that had formed and had been cheering and shouting suddenly fell silent.

"Abby! What the smeck are *you* doing? I thought you liked *me*?" Alex begged, barely able to believe what was happening.

Abby's expression was one of confusion and surprise.

"What are you talking about?" she asked. She looked as if she wanted to say more, but Iggy interrupted.

"Ignore him, Abby. You know Franklin's a total dexter," he said, his lips curled up in a sneer as he put his arm around Abby's shoulders and steered her up the steps and into the school.

Chapter Ten
Tom's Odd Turn

The crowd started to disperse, chattering animatedly and casting curious glances back at Alex, who continued to struggle against Tom and Sol. In spite of Alex's efforts to free himself, his two friends hung on, pinning his arms to his sides. Alex fought for several more seconds, his fury still possessing him, until Iggy and Abby entered the gleaming building.

All the anger and adrenaline suddenly drained from him as they disappeared from view. He slumped forward, feeling sapped of all energy. He no longer felt the desire to fight or free himself or do ... anything.

Realizing their friend had lost his bloodlust and regained his self-control, Sol and Tom let him go and Alex stepped away from them, wiping his mouth with his shirt sleeve as he did so and noticing a thin line of blood. Now his passion had passed, he felt his lips and ear start to throb with pain from Iggy's punches.

"What was all that about, Alex? Are you crazy?" Sol asked, forehead creased with concern as he panted from the exertion of holding back his friend.

"What do you mean, crazy? You would have done the same thing if you caught someone who'd just asked you out kissing someone else!"

"Just asked you out?" Tom asked, eyebrows raised.

"Yes, Tom. I had a date with Abby on Friday night. She was going to ... well, I think she might have wanted to be my girlfriend," he added.

Tom and Sol exchanged confused glances, but Alex persisted.

"Guys, she asked me out on this very spot after school on Friday. You were both with me. Don't you remember?"

"No, I don't remember. Alex, she's been with Iggy for six months," Sol said, shaking his head and looking more worried than ever.

"Sol's right," Tom chimed in before Alex could reply. "Abby is Iggy's girl. You know that. We *all* know that. And we're all jealous. But what do you expect? The Iggys of the world always get the girl. Even if he is a smeckin' braggster," Tom spat.

Alex shook his head, still unable to understand. Was the whole world going mad? Or was it just him? Could he have imagined his time with Abby last Friday? What was *happening*?

"You don't look so good, Alex," Sol said, interrupting his thoughts.

"Sol's right," Tom added. "Come on, let's get you cleaned up before class starts. Sol, can you run ahead? Tell Ms. Monroe that Alex fell and we might be a couple of minutes late. Alex, I'll come with you to the bathroom, help get you tidied up."

Sol nodded and ran into the school. Alex and Tom went more slowly, passing up the now empty entrance and into the pristine corridors. Alex's ear—the one Iggy had thumped—was throbbing, causing Alex to hear an odd buzzing sound. His mouth hurt and he could taste the blood. The knuckles on his right hand, the one he'd used to punch his rival, stung.

Soon the two boys were in the nearest bathroom. Alex began to clean himself up, washing the blood out of his mouth and using the mirror to help him flatten down his hair and straighten his clothes, which looked pretty disheveled after the brawl. Tom stood by, watching his friend in concerned silence.

Satisfied he no longer looked like a kid who'd been on the wrong end of a beatdown, Alex exited the bathroom, Tom following.

They had just rounded a corner and were approaching their classroom when Alex stopped and turned to his friend.

"You sure I look okay now?" he asked, seeking a final validation before his teacher and classmates saw him.

"Yes, Alexander. But I must raise another issue with you, an issue of some significance," Tom replied slowly. There was something odd in Tom's voice that made Alex stop short.

"Are you okay, Tom? You sound ... I don't know ... weird," Alex said, looking more closely at his friend.

"I am quite satisfactory, thank you. But I would like to make a suggestion. I think you should have your MeChip examined."

"What? Why?"

"I suspect there is something amiss with it."

"What makes you say that, Tom?" Alex asked, still gazing at his friend in consternation. Something definitely felt wrong here, Alex decided. Tom never spoke this formally. And his tone was off—almost robotic, without his usual spark or jaunty breeziness. His eyes had a glassy, unfocused look. With a jolt of alarm, Alex realized his friend had stopped blinking.

"I wonder if there is a connection between your MeChip and what just occurred with Abby. Could it be possible?"

"No, not really, Tom. You know MeChips are foolproof," Alex replied dismissively. "Anyway, it has a self-sensor that would tell me if anything was wrong."

"Even so, I would highly recommend it."

"But why?" Alex persisted, still unsettled by Tom's odd, stilted manner.

"I cannot explain at this time. Just promise you will take my advice, Alexander. Please."

"Okay. I mean, I guess. But seriously, Tom, you sound really weird. Are you sure you're alright?"

Tom did not respond straight away. His head slumped slightly, almost as if he was falling asleep standing up. Then, as quickly as it had happened, Tom seemed to jerk back to life.

"What's that, Alex? What were we talking about?" he asked, the old light back in his eyes. "Oh, never mind. Here's the classroom. Come on, let's get inside. I hope old Monroe doesn't give us a detention for being late!"

Chapter Eleven
The Happy Store

The sun blazed down on the empty exterior of the school, reflecting brightly off chrome, glass and steel. Silence reigned, with not even a whisper of wind to stir the leaves on this hot, breathless afternoon.

The bell rang to signal the end of the day, breaking the silence with its insistent sound. Moments later, the front doors burst open and waves of students surged out, talking, shouting and laughing as they cascaded down the steps and into the parking lot and the streets. Only when the crowd had begun to thin a little did Alex finally emerge, flanked by Sol and Tom.

Alex's mood, which had been foul earlier in the day, had barely improved. He had been unable to shake off the horrible image of Iggy kissing Abby. The pain in his mouth, ear and hand hadn't helped. Neither had the smirks and whispers that had followed him down the corridors as news of his fight with—and defeat by—Iggy spread through the school like wildfire. Then there was Tom's weird behavior in the corridor.

To make matters worse, their plans to rehearse for the Best Band contest had failed. First, Alex's efforts to book a rehearsal room had been unsuccessful since the music rooms had all been snagged by other bands. Secondly, Sol's attempt to persuade Alex's mom to let them rehearse after school had fallen on deaf ears. While Alex knew his mom liked Sol and saw him as a "good influence," she would not be moved, apparently telling Sol that Alex "knew what he had to do" to make things right again. The only silver lining was Alex had managed to book one of the music rooms for lunchtime tomorrow, so at least they'd have somewhere to practice the following day.

"Okay, so we're going to the Happy Store, then. Is that the plan?" Sol asked as they walked down the steps and past the school gates.

"Yes," Alex replied.

"And you think it's worth the risk?" Sol asked, frowning.

"It'll only take a few minutes. Besides, it's virtually on my way home. My mom won't even notice," Alex said defensively.

"Are you sure?" Tom asked. "I mean, I'm all for taking risks, you know that. But your mom told you to go straight home after school and we need you back on her good side for the sake of the band!"

"Hey, you were the one who suggested I go there!" Alex protested. "You told me to get my MeChip checked, remember?"

"Did I?" Tom replied, scratching his chin. For a moment he looked confused. Then his face brightened.

"I can check out the new synthi-snare drum that just came in!"

"And I can try the updated Mark 4 Laser Bass Guitar," Sol added. "I'm curious how it compares to my trusty old Mark 2."

They made their way quickly down the street, each of them thinking about what they'd do at the Happy Store. After a minute's silence, though, Tom spoke again:

"Hey, I wonder if that new girl from history class will be there? She's *so* tidy!" he said, grinning.

"What?" Tom asked a second later as Sol rolled his eyes. "She said she was looking to buy a new microphone, so she *might* be there."

As if on cue, they turned another corner and saw the Happy Store ahead of them. They stepped towards it and the enormous doors swooshed open automatically, admitting them into an enormous, crowded space teeming with customers. Above the throng, Alex noticed the ever-present holo-neon sign and its cheery welcome: "The Happy Store—Home of the MeChip and More!" Smiley faces surrounded the glowing, 3-D words.

The Happy Store was a regular haunt for the three music lovers. Alex had decided long ago that it was an *uber* hangout spot, with its neo-café, plastilux couches, extensive music section and latest Happy Corps tech gear all packed into one gleaming, airy, futuristic space.

"See, I told you she'd be here," Tom whispered, nudging Sol and nodding towards a brown-haired teenaged girl dressed in pleth boots, biz-hippie jeans and a neochromal top, her back to them as she inspected a new mike. "Come on."

Tom and Sol started to thread their way through the crowd towards the music area and the new girl, barely noticing as Alex bid them a hasty goodbye and made his way to the tech support area at the back of the store.

The press of people thinned as Alex approached the least cool part of the shop, where three tech staff propped up the counter, idling the time away. Evidently, they didn't have much to do. Alex wasn't surprised, since Happy Corps products had a reputation for reliability that was second-to-none.

The techies looked surprised as Alex stepped forward, as if they were affronted that anyone would need their assistance. All three stared at him, but none of them spoke.

"Um, could I get your help with something?" Alex asked, breaking the awkward silence.

"Probably," one of them replied arrogantly. The other two smirked.

"It's my MeChip," Alex persisted uncomfortably.

"What about it?"

"I think there might be something wrong it."

"Has the self-sensor activated?"

"No."

"Then what are you worried about? The sensor will tell you if there's a problem." Dismissing Alex with one final, withering look, the techie turned back to his friends and resumed their low-pitched conversation.

Inwardly cursing them out for being such total dexters, Alex gave it one last try.

"I *know* the self-sensor should have activated, but I just have a feeling something's wrong. Can you do me a favor and take a look?"

"Fine!" sighed the techie reluctantly, shaking his head and looking at Alex as if he was a deeply unintelligent amoeba. "But you're wasting your time. These things are foolproof. They *never* break." The other two techies nodded.

"I understand. But still ..." Alex persisted.

"Alright. Come back into the workshop then, if you must."

While the other two shop assistants continued their conversation, this one led Alex through a rear doorway and into a windowless, dimly-lit room with a bunch of technical gear all around the walls. One machine—a large, slender grey box towards the back—had the words "MeChip Diagnostics" written on it in large letters. The techie pointed to a seat in front.

"Sit down here, please. Ever had your MeChip tested before?" he asked, peering at a small screen above several buttons.

"No."

"Okay, well I warn you it's going to feel a little weird. First, I need to unzip your skin so the MeChip is fully visible. It shouldn't hurt," he added, seeing the look of worry on Alex's face.

The techie swiveled the chair around and Alex felt fingers pulling at the back of his neck, then a small tug as he took a hold of the tiny zip that held a small fold of his skin in place. For a moment, Alex experienced an almost irresistible urge to pull away, to protect his MeChip, which was concealed beneath his skin and held in place by the zip. This, he knew, had been attached in a quick and painless MeChip implanting procedure when he was just an infant. There, at the top of his spine, was this shiny, circular wonder of modern technology. Teeming with state-of-the art circuitry, it was about the size of a dollar coin, with the words "The Little Chip That Does It All" etched in miniature letters around the outside.

To Alex, it felt like a deep invasion of his privacy to have someone messing around with his most important possession; like being seen naked emerging from the shower or having one's personal diary read out loud to strangers.

"You're not going to take it out are you?" Alex asked anxiously.

"No," the techie reassured him. "It just needs to be visible for our diagnostic laser."

"Okay, here goes," the man added, pulling out a small, electronic device with a thin infrared beam projecting from one end. "I'm going to scan your MeChip now. It'll tickle a little, but that's all. Just hold still for a few seconds."

Alex tried not to move while his MeChip was scanned. The techie was right; it felt like someone was blowing gently on the back of his neck. An odd feeling, but not painful. After a few seconds, the man put the scanner back in its holder and Alex felt the techie's fingers on his neck once more as he zipped the attachable flap of skin back in place.

"What happens now?" Alex asked, curious.

"The results will show up on my MeChip retina display in a moment. Okay, here goes—"

"How's it look?" Alex asked, impatient to know the results.

"All perfectly normal," he replied casually. "It's like I said, your sensor would show up anything unusual. Yours is just a standard, beautiful MeChip, the most perfectly-crafted piece of technology ever invented. You see, you were wasting your time," he added smugly.

"Okay, well thanks anyway," Alex replied. He stood up and was about to leave when the techie spoke again, stopping Alex in his tracks.

"Wait. That's odd. Really odd!"

"What?"

"Well ... no. That can't be right," he continued.

"What? Tell me!" Alex said, starting to worry.

"It looks like your MeChip's been hacked. That's really, really unusual! More than unusual. It should be impossible. I've never seen anything like this before," said the techie, forehead creasing. For a moment, neither of them spoke. "I'd better get my manager," the man said finally, walking back towards the door.

To Alex's surprise, though, the man suddenly stopped. His head drooped onto his chest and his arms fell limply by his sides. For several seconds he was completely still. Finally, he spoke.

"I have changed my mind. There is nothing the manager needs to know. I cannot help you," he intoned, his voice a quiet monotone.

"What? But you just said—"

"I said I cannot help you, Alexander. You should visit the old tech store on the edge of town. Only they can help you now."

"What are you talking about? What old store?" Alex asked, confused.

"The one near Bright Green Mining. It's always been there. You just have to look. It is called John Locke's Indie Tech Shop. You should go there instead. You *must*."

Before Alex could ask any more questions the techie shuddered and lifted his head with a jerk. He stood staring at Alex for several seconds, blinking rapidly and looking confused, as if unsure where he was. Finally, his eyes regained their focus.

"What's that? Where were we? Oh yeah, your MeChip. Like I said, there's nothing wrong with it."

"Wait ... what? Are you sure?" Alex asked, now feeling thoroughly perplexed.

"Oh yeah, yeah. These things never go wrong. You're fine."

"So, I don't need to go to the other shop? The independent tech shop you mentioned?"

"What's that?"

"The indie tech shop. Remember?"

"What are you talking about?" the techie asked, looking as confused as Alex.

"Oh ... nothing. Thanks," Alex mumbled, giving up.

The two of them left the room and the techie rejoined his colleagues behind the counter. Alex heard the techie whisper something to his friends, who looked at Alex and laughed conspiratorially, heads close together. Feeling more mystified than ever, Alex started to work his way back through the crowd. He saw Sol and Tom talking with the brown-haired girl by the microphones. From his animated movements Alex guessed Tom was in the middle of delivering a joke, although Alex couldn't tell if the others were amused. Sol was frowning and shaking his head, while the girl had her arms crossed and was definitely *not* smiling. Realizing he would be late home if he stayed any longer, Alex left them to it, leaving the store through the giant doors and emerging into the heat and sunlight.

As he hurried down the street towards his house, he felt, if anything, even more baffled than before. What had just happened to that techie? Had the guy been messing with Alex to impress his friends? If so, why did his odd behavior and his abrupt change in personality seem a lot like Tom's earlier in the day? And what about the independent tech store the guy had mentioned. Should he go check it out?

So many questions. But no answers. None at all. The truth still seemed maddeningly out of reach.

Chapter Twelve
Guitar Playoff

Alex was still no closer to a decision when he awoke the next morning. He had checked out John Locke's Indie Tech Shop on his MeMap that evening—luckily, maps were one of the few features not affected by the parental override on his MeChip—and been surprised at the result.

He'd started by opening his MeMap—which he could pull up directly on his retina with voice or mind command—over the Bright Green Mining Company. This was a big factory on the other side of town that the Happy Store techie had said was close to the indie tech shop. Sure enough, Bright Green Mining was on the map—a large, square space that covered several blocks on the edge of town. At first, Alex couldn't locate the tech store, even though he honed in and looked at all the surrounding shops and buildings carefully. He had been about to give up when he'd decided as a last resort to request the place by name. Initially, the search function on his MeMap returned "No result" on his retina display. Then the text had flickered for a moment before apparently changing its mind, confirming the name and locking on its coordinates a moment later.

Just as the techie had said, there *was* a place called John Locke's Indie Tech Shop close to the Bright Green Mining factory. It looked tiny on the overhead map, a sliver of space sandwiched between the factory and a café called Dave's Diner. When Alex had switched his MeMap to street view mode, the shop looked even smaller, just a hole-in-the-wall with a narrow door and a tiny window made of frosted glass.

Still, it was definitely real. The question was: should he go? And if he did, *when* should he go? As his mom and dad kept reminding him, he was still grounded. Unlike the Happy Store, this John Locke Tech place was not on his route home but on the far side of town. Not close at all. How could he go there and not get busted? It was yet another problem without any obvious answer.

When he arrived at his classroom five minutes before the start of school, Sol and Tom were already sitting in their usual spots.

"We were just talking about yesterday's fiasco at the Happy Shop," Sol said as Alex sat down.

"Oh yeah? What happened?" Alex asked, curious.

"Tom made an *uber* dexter of himself with the girl from history class."

"Her name's Denise and I did *not* make a dexter of myself," Tom replied defensively, arms crossed.

"Yeah, you did," Sol said smugly.

"What makes you say that?"

"Well, let me see. First, she didn't laugh at any of your jokes."

"She *did* laugh," Tom said.

"Only when you tripped over the mike cables. That doesn't count."

"Alright, what else?"

"Secondly, she didn't like your drumming on that new synth-kit."

"She never said that!" Tom objected.

"Dude, she walked off while you were still performing."

"That doesn't prove anything! She might have ... I don't know ... got a MeChip message from her mom or something."

"Okay, well what about the fact that when you asked her out, she said no?"

"I didn't ask her out. Well ... not exactly."

"You asked her if she'd like to go to a movie sometime."

"Yeah, but I didn't specify that it would be with *me*. I was just curious if she liked movies in general!" Tom replied, his usually pale face now turning bright red. "Plus, she didn't say no."

"Yeah, she did."

"No. She said no, *thanks*! Which is a lot more polite," Tom said, his voice getting quieter with every word.

"Oh, of course. Totally different!" Sol remarked with a smirk.

There was silence for a moment before Tom spoke again.

"So Alex, how did it go with your MeChip check-up?" he asked, changing the subject.

"Oh, it was alright," Alex replied evasively, still strangely reluctant to talk about his problems even with his best friends. "I might take it to another place for a second opinion, though. Have you guys heard of John Locke's Indie Tech Shop?"

"John's what-now shop?" Sol asked, raising an eyebrow.

"John Locke's Indie Tech Shop. It's on the other side of town, apparently. Near Bright Green Mining."

"No," Tom and Sol replied together. "Are you sure that's its name?" Sol continued. "I mean, I know all the techie hangouts and I've never heard of it."

"You know *all* the hangouts do you?" Tom asked.

"Yeah. And my cousin lives near Bright Green Mining, so I think I'd have seen it."

"Dexter!" Tom muttered under his breath, clearly still smarting from Sol's teasing about Denise.

"What?" Sol asked.

"Nothing!" Tom replied. "You should go check it out, Alex. I mean, what harm can it do?"

"None, I suppose. I guess I'll think about it."

"On more important matters, don't forget we've got the main music room booked for our practice this lunchtime. I can't wait to bust out the school's new synthi-drum set," Tom said, sounding a little more like his usual, upbeat self.

Just then their teacher entered the room.

"Alright, people, your attention please! Please pull up Thomas Paine's *Common Sense* on your MeChips. Some people believe the American Revolution would not have succeeded without this document."

"Why, Ms. Monroe?" asked a kid in the front row.

"I'm glad you asked, Mr. Witherspoon. Well, we know from people's diaries and newspapers from the time that his book turned the tide of popular opinion quickly and emphatically away from the British and towards the revolutionaries at a crucial moment. The year, of course, was 1776 ..."

A few hours later, Alex, Tom and Sol entered an empty classroom and closed the door on a corridor crowded with noisy schoolmates making their way to the cafeteria for lunch.

The room boasted an array of impressive, ultra-modern musical equipment. To Alex, it looked like no expense had been spared. As he surveyed this Aladdin's cave of tuneful treasures, Alex's eyes passed fleetingly over a funny-looking mannequin hanging from the far wall. It was dressed in jeans, boots, a white t-shirt and leather jacket. A dusty old X-shaped guitar was strapped around its shoulders. Ignoring this relic from a bygone age, the friends spread out, grabbing the best new gear. They were soon set up and were about to launch into a tune when the door burst open and Iggy and his bandmates strode in. The tall, handsome young man looked down at them, a sneering expression on his face.

"Well, well, well, what have we here? The three worst musicians in the school all in one room. Oh, and Mr. X the mannequin! Hey Mr.

X, if they ask you to join their band, turn them down. You may be a stuffed dummy with an obsolete instrument, but you're still too good for this rabble! Am I right, Mr. X?"

Iggy and his cronies burst into raucous laughter while behind them several of their classmates stopped and started crowding around the door, curious to see what was going down.

"We've booked this room for our band practice, Iggy. You've no right to be here," Alex said defensively.

"Go on, then, practice. I'm not stopping you," Iggy replied, still smirking as he sidled further into the room.

Alex looked at Tom and Sol, who seemed as uncertain as he was how to respond. Sol lifted his shoulders in a shrug and Tom looked down at the floor as snickers and whispers came from the crowd gathering by the door.

"Lost for words again, Alex? You're really making a habit of this. Come on, give me the guitar. I'll show you how a real musician plays," Iggy said, reaching out to grab the instrument.

Iggy's actions seemed to trigger something in Alex, who shifted his grip on the guitar, taking its neck in both hands and brandishing it in front of him like a weapon, ready to swing it if his enemy came a step closer.

"Calm down, dexter," Iggy said coolly as he shrugged and turned away from Alex, who stood there uncertainly. Casually, Iggy began walking around the room, inspecting the other instruments and ignoring his adversary completely. Still unsure what to do, Alex finally decided to press on with their practice. He began to strum the guitar, diffidently playing a few chords. Meanwhile, Iggy had picked out a second guitar from the rack, along with a large amp—or amplifier—which acted as a loud speaker for the instrument. Plugging it in, he turned up the volume on the amp and started to play over Alex, drowning out his foe's music in a tidal wave of aggressive but catchy chords.

"You're doing it all wrong, Alex. This is how you play!" Iggy shouted above the sound as the small crowd spilled through the doorway and entered the room, cheering and clapping his performance.

Alex tried to ignore him, but when Iggy turned the volume up still further, Alex was forced to stop in mid-strum, looking up angrily at his rival.

Iggy stood there, feet wide apart, staring at Alex with that irritating, mocking smile, as if he knew he was the better player.

It was clearly a challenge and Alex felt his heart begin to race. Along with his sudden spike in anxiety, however, Alex also felt a surge of adrenaline and anger. He reached down to his own amp, turned up the volume, and replied with a riff of his own; a series of intricate, cleverly-woven chords. To Alex's surprise, a few of the crowd applauded as he paused and stared back at his rival, chin held high.

"So it's a playoff you want, huh?" Iggy said. "Why don't I go first?" he added. Without waiting for an answer, Iggy performed a complex series of chords, his fingers moving deftly over the frets. After a few seconds he stopped and looked up at his adversary.

Alex knew the rules of the game. First, he must repeat what Iggy had played, then add something of his own. Iggy, in turn, would play the whole sequence back—both his own and Alex's parts—then add something on top of this. Alex would reply, adding still more. The contest would continue until someone forgot the right sequence. And lost. Alex paused a moment, trying to recall Iggy's chords perfectly.

"Giving up already, dexter?" Iggy said, still smirking.

"You wish!" Alex shot back. He played back Iggy's chords, then added two more of his own.

"Is that the best you can do?" Iggy sneered.

He repeated both his and Alex's chords perfectly, then added more of *his* own. Alex replied, throwing in a couple of tricky and unexpected minor chords. The crowd murmured and cheered as Iggy and Alex went back and forth. Iggy was sweating now, his brow creased in concentration as he tried to get the sequence just right.

Now it was Alex's turn. He was going to get it perfectly and would add something really tricky to trip Iggy up, he thought. Maybe, just maybe, he could win this thing. He was just starting to repeat the sequence from the start when Iggy interrupted.

"You'll never get it, Alex. Just give up like you did last year. Abby and I both agree you're a loser."

Abby. The name threw him, knocking him off his stride. Like a cross-country runner who trips on a tree root, Alex's fingers stumbled on the strings, he missed one chord, then another before stopping abruptly.

Instantly, Iggy started playing again, repeating the sequence perfectly before adding a great little addition at the end. He had won. The crowd whooped and cheered.

"And that's how it's done! Once a dexter, always a dexter, Franklin. I can't wait for the Best Band contest. It'll be fun to see you freeze in front of the whole school again. Honestly, you seem to love being humiliated."

Iggy placed the school guitar carefully back in its rack, stowed the amp below a shelf, and strutted out the door, flanked by his cronies and fans, who clapped him on the back as he sauntered out into the corridor, turning in the direction of the cafeteria and leaving Alex, Tom and Sol alone once more.

"Not again," Alex muttered to himself, burying his face in his hands.

"Don't take it too badly, Alex. He wouldn't have won if he hadn't broken your concentration, which is definitely not fair. You had him on the ropes and he knew it," Sol said, patting him on the back.

"Sol's right, Alex. You've just got to ignore him. Come on, let's practice," Tom added. As he was speaking, he strode over to the door, shut it, and locked it from the inside for good measure. "At least we won't be interrupted now."

There was a long silence. With an effort, Alex pulled himself together and tried to shake off the deep depression that had descended on him as Sol counted them in and they started their rehearsal in earnest.

Chapter Thirteen
The Last Straw

Alex was still feeling downcast as the day drew to an end. He had been forced to endure more stares and whispered conversations behind his back in the classrooms and corridors as word of his latest defeat spread. Nothing Sol and Tom could say or do really helped.

As soon as the bell rang for the end of school Alex had rushed straight home, not minding that he was grounded and quite happy, in fact, for a chance to be alone. In an effort to distract himself he had completed all his homework, although it hadn't been easy to concentrate with so many other thoughts swirling around his brain. After finishing his work he'd spent half an hour just lying on his bed and trying to process all that had happened.

Things had started to go wrong after that wonderful evening with Abby, he realized. First there was the nightmare of Abby's father spitting up blood; then those mysterious figures taking her dad's body and the weird fact no one seemed to realize he'd been replaced with a substitute.

That was the worst of it, he knew. Compared to that, he supposed the fact Abby was suddenly dating Iggy, or that Iggy had publicly shamed him, Alex, twice were minor matters. Not that they felt minor to Alex, of course. But he knew they were small fry when set beside what he was pretty sure had been the death of a neighbor.

To top it all off, there had been this whole weirdness with people's personalities seeming to change. First it was Tom, then that techie at the Happy Store. That was hard to explain, too. So was Tom's suggestion there might be something wrong with his MeChip, and this whole business about John Locke's Indie Tech Store.

But no matter how many times he replayed these events in his mind, Alex still couldn't put things together in a way that made any sense. It was like trying to construct a 5000-piece jigsaw puzzle without knowing what the original picture looked like and with a bunch of the pieces missing, plus pieces from other puzzles mixed in, too. Perhaps, he decided as his father called him down for dinner, he should try to forget about it all. Keep his head down and stay out of trouble.

Although he was still grounded, it was pretty obvious to Alex that his parents were no longer giving him the silent treatment. This was a relief, until they started asking about his day.

"Did you have band practice at lunchtime?" his mother asked as they started on their lasagne.

"Yeah."

"How was it?"

"Okay," Alex replied, trying to sound casual as he resisted the urge to tell them about his run-in with Iggy.

"I'm glad you're practicing, Alex. I still think you can win the Best Band contest."

"Thanks, Mom. Would you consider letting me practice after school, then? That would help a lot."

"No, Alex. You know what you need to do for that to happen."

He did know, of course. He'd need to apologize for the events of the weekend. Although he wanted his freedom, however, he wasn't yet ready to apologize for something he *knew* wasn't his fault. There was an awkward silence for a few seconds before his father finally changed the subject.

"Hey hon," he said, turning to Alex's mom, "did you catch the news about Secretary of State Kirchner? Looks like the trade embargo with the United States of Europe isn't going to end anytime soon. He's still trying to get the English to come off the fence, of course," he continued animatedly, clearly interested in discussing the political news of the day. That didn't interest Alex much, who tuned out and turned back to his own thoughts once more.

After dinner, Alex was getting up and about to go back to his room when his mother spoke to him again.

"Alex, can you take out the trash, please."

"Sure," he replied, grabbing a big plastic bag and lugging it out the front door. He was just a couple of steps away from the nearest trash can, which was placed near the corner of the property where it connected with Abby's garden, when he caught sight of movement in the shadows of a nearby tree.

"Who's there?" he said, peering into the darkness.

To his surprise, Iggy stepped out, followed a couple of seconds later by Abby. She wiped her mouth with her fingers and Alex had the horrible impression that they had probably just been making out.

"Franklin ... you again!" Iggy said in his usual, arrogant drawl.

Alex fought the urge to vault the fence and punch his despised nemesis in the face. Instead, he lifted the lid on the garbage can, dumped the plastic bag inside, and closed it as the two of them watched him in silence. He was about to turn his back on them and return to the house without another word, when Abby spoke.

"Alex, I don't know what happened yesterday, but don't do anything like that again, okay?" she said quietly.

"You don't know what happened yesterday? Seriously? Well, then, I'm not going to remind you," he said, turning away from them and walking as quickly as he could back to his house. His blood felt like it was boiling and there was a strange swirling sound in his head, as if he was underwater.

"Can you believe that guy? What a smeckin' dexter! I'm sorry for you that you have him as a neighbor, Abby. Honestly!"

Alex couldn't help but hear Iggy's cruel words as he walked away. A moment later, he had pushed open the door and stepped inside, slamming it shut behind him. Too late, he wondered what Abby would say to Iggy in reply. Now he'd never know.

"Everything alright?" his mother asked as he re-entered the kitchen.

"Yes," Alex lied. "I'm going up to my room, okay?"

"Sure, Alex."

"Don't forget to finish your homework," his dad said, looking up from the sink where he was busy washing the dishes.

"Already did."

"Really? Okay, Alex. Well ... keep it up!" his dad said, looking surprised but pleased.

As soon as Alex got back to his bedroom, he picked up his guitar once more, strummed a few angry chords, then put it down again. It was no good, he thought. He couldn't let this go. His whole life had been turned upside down, his nerves were shattered and he was more than halfway to believing he was going mad. As an image of Iggy and Abby locked in a passionate embrace came unbidden into his brain, Alex made a firm promise to himself; he was going to get to the bottom of all this, even if it was the last thing he did.

Chapter Fourteen
John Locke's Indie Tech Shop

Alex stopped to get his bearings. Although his MeMap had guided him perfectly to the right spot, he did not know this part of town very well and found himself feeling oddly out of place.

As he stood there uncertainly, he felt a slight chill in the air, a light breeze bringing the barest hint of the changing seasons. Soon, September would slip into October, leaves would start to fall and summer's heat would be just a memory.

He had left school early, taking advantage of the fact his last class that day was a free study period. If he hurried, he could visit John Locke's Indie Tech Shop and still get home before his mom. She need never know where he'd been.

Now he was here, though, he was having second thoughts. Across the street, the whole block was dominated by a sleek, modern building. With its gleaming windows, oversized-solar panels, and two large, tan-colored chimneys sprouting out like enormous, branchless trees, it looked like a cross between a modern office complex and a futuristic, ecofriendly factory. Above the opulent marble entrance, a giant, glistening sign proudly proclaimed: "Bright Green Mining—A Happy Corps Company".

Meanwhile, a steady trickle of Happy Corps employees entered and exited through the front doors, talking, smiling and generally lending an air of bustling conviviality to the whole scene. As he watched them come and go Alex couldn't help but smile, too; it looked like a great place to work.

His grin faded, though, as he turned his gaze once more towards the little store that lay in Bright Green Mining's shadow. John Locke's Indie Tech Shop did *not* look like a great place to work or even to visit, come to that. It was decidedly run down and tatty when compared with its grandiose neighbor that dominated this wide, tree-lined avenue. The paint on the little tech shop's door was peeling. The single, small window was coated in dust and had a crack in the top right corner. The place looked decidedly *out* of place, like a nasty speck of dirt on a freshly-laundered towel.

Other people on the avenue clearly shared Alex's point of view, for the place attracted not a shred of interest from passersby. No one entered or left as Alex continued to loiter and stare at it from across the street. In fact, no one paid it any attention at all. Alex wondered if they were deliberately ignoring it: whether they, too, felt it brought down the "tone" of the neighborhood. It was hardly an inviting place—a little creepy in fact—and he wondered idly how such a poorly-maintained business had kept itself going when the Happy Store and other, much nicer tech shops were around. Not for the first time, Alex wondered if coming here was really such a good idea.

It was only when he noticed the large clock on the side of the Bright Green Mining building strike 3:00 p.m. that he realized he needed to hurry. Reluctantly, he approached the crosswalk, waited for the pedestrian light to turn green, and hurried across. Once again, he stopped and stood outside the door, still disinclined to enter. A couple of pedestrians glanced at him as he hesitated on the front step. Finally, he squared his shoulders, reached for the handle, and went inside.

It was not what he'd expected. Unlike its exterior, the inside was clean and tidy, with neat rows of tech gear on shelves around the walls. As his eyes adjusted to the soft lighting, he saw that most of the gear was antique, with archaic computers, games consoles, cassette recorders, and other electronic memorabilia from a bygone age. The shop had an old-fashioned but not uncomfortable feel. The one jarring note was that there seemed to be no one there, neither customers nor staff.

Alex's attention was drawn to a flatscreen television—the type that had been rendered instantly obsolete when the MeChip came out more than 20 years ago. The television was fixed to a wall. Remarkably, it was actually working and Alex watched with interest as a Fennec News anchor, whom he vaguely recognized from his MeChip, reported the day's political events:

"Meanwhile, President Donaldson was at Camp David for the Great Powers meeting with the Chinese and Russian premiers, while Secretary of State Kirchner met with England's Prime Minister in London to discuss their long-awaited free trade agreement as the war of words with the United States of Europe continues..."

"Here you are at last. You took your time, young man."

The words snapped Alex back to reality and he spun around looking for the source of the voice.

An elderly man had emerged from an interior door at the back of the shop. In one hand he was holding a transistor radio—the type Alex had once seen in a museum—while in the other was a screwdriver. The man was wearing a vintage, collared white shirt and a blue tie. He was short, slim and slightly stooped, with thinning grey hair and a short, trim white beard. At first sight, just an ordinary, elderly person.

Except for his eyes. These were of the most startling green, piercing and intelligent and active. He was staring intently at Alex, a look of keen interest on his lined face.

"Oh ... um ... excuse me, sir. Is this John Locke's Indie Tech Shop?" Alex asked.

"Of course," the man nodded in a gravelly voice, still gazing at Alex in a way he found somewhat unnerving.

"And do you ... I mean, do you check MeChips here?" Alex continued uncertainly.

"No, we do not check MeChips."

"Oh," said Alex, feeling confused. "Well, I'm sorry to have troubled you," he added, turning towards the door. As he reached for the handle, he felt ... what? Relief, certainly, at leaving the company of this strange old man. But what else? Disappointment? Yes, he decided, disappointment his trip had been a failure.

"I do not check MeChips," the old man repeated in a louder voice as Alex paused, his fingers still around the door handle, "but I can certainly help you with your problem."

"Um, well, I really just need my MeChip checking," Alex replied, turning to face the man once more.

"We both know that is untrue. You should stay, Alex. I may be unwilling to check your MeChip, but I *can* reveal the truth and help you understand what is happening to you," he said, a thin smile playing across his lips.

"How do you know my name?" Alex asked suspiciously.

"How do I know your name? Oh, that is simple, Alex. I know your name in the same way I know what really happened with Abby's father and who those people were who took him away."

"You know about that?" Alex asked, almost unable to believe his ears.

"Of course. I know everything, Alex. I know what happened between you and Abby last Friday night. I know of your belief that Abby's father has been replaced. I know of your visit to the Happy Store to have your MeChip checked. I know about your friend Tom's strange behavior. I even know about you being grounded."

Alex was so shocked he couldn't speak. But the old man wasn't done yet.

"More important than all this, though, I know *why* all these things have happened. Do you want to know why, Alex?"

"Um ... I guess so."

"You guess so?"

"No ... I mean yes, I want to know why these things are happening," Alex said, his palms feeling suddenly sweaty as he rubbed them nervously.

"And what would you like to know first?" the old man asked, his voice still quiet and matter-of-fact, as if they were just talking about the weather.

"Well ... um ... how come no else saw what I saw last weekend? I mean, why did no one else see Abby's dad cough up blood."

"Oh, that is an easy one, Alex. You saw it because I allowed you to see it. Because I can control it."

"You mean you're the one who did that to him?" Alex asked, taking a step back in shock. "But that's horrible!"

"That's not what I meant, Alex," the man replied, still calm. "But I *could* have done something like it if I'd wished. I can do anything to anyone. Even you, Alex. What you see, what you hear, even what you think. I can control it."

"But that's illegal," Alex said, his mind racing. "You're probably ... I don't know ... a criminal. Or you're crazy. Either way, I'm calling the Regs," he said, realizing this man needed to be stopped.

Alex summoned the emergency number for the Regs—the 'cops' as his parents still quaintly called them—on his MeChip. His brain instructed the number to dial and a moment later his ears heard the tone ringing. After a second, though, it abruptly hung up.

That was weird, he thought. Perhaps he'd done something wrong?

He tried a second time. Again, the same thing happened. His call to the Regs would not go through.

Panicking, he took another step towards the door, at the same time looking back at the old man.

It was then he noticed the man had put down the radio and screwdriver. Instead, he was holding a small device, like an old television remote. And he was pointing it at Alex.

In desperation, Alex tried calling the Regs a third time, still watching the old man closely. The call began as before, then cut out again just as the old man clicked a button on his device. There was no doubt at all in Alex's mind that this stranger had somehow canceled his call. The man looked at him, his hand still holding the small remote, his face still impassive, still impossible to read.

"That can't happen," Alex muttered, shaking his head. "No one can interfere with a MeChip."

"Really, Alex. Are you sure?"

"Yes! First, because it's impossible to hack the most secure technology ever invented. Secondly, because it's illegal. And thirdly, because you'd get caught!"

"You think so?" the man asked, sounding bemused.

"I know so! Happy Corps has the best techies in the land. They'd catch anyone messing with the MeChip in no time, especially an old dexter like you," Alex said defiantly.

"Then how did I prevent your call?" the man asked, smiling grimly. "Alex, please stop this nonsense and allow me to explain."

"Explain what?" Alex shot back as his growing fear gave way to anger. "Explain how you're illegally blocking my calls? Explain how you seem to be spying on me so you know every detail of my life, even things my own parents don't? Explain how you know about Abby's dad dying. I don't need your explanations!" Alex said, his voice shaking.

The man just looked at Alex, his expression cool and unruffled.

"I bet you killed him, didn't you? I bet you killed Abby's father," Alex said as a terrible suspicion entered his mind. Again, the man's expression barely changed, although his eyes narrowed just a fraction.

"You need locking up, you old devil!" Alex blurted out, his anger and his fear still fighting for the upper hand.

"Are you quite finished?" the man asked, his voice quiet and measured.

Deciding he needed to leave this strange shop and its stranger occupant, Alex shot one last, venomous look at the green-eyed man before turning on his heel and reaching for the door.

"Don't leave, Alexander!" the man said, raising his voice at last. "Calm down and let me explain. Don't make me show you the hard way."

"Oh, so you're threatening me now, huh? Well, no way am I staying with a smeckin' Crazy-Clinton like you. I'm outta here," Alex hurled back, not even looking over his shoulder as he reached for the door handle, tugged it open, and stepped out into the busy street.

"Then you leave me no choice," the man replied, speaking so quietly now that Alex barely heard him above the noise of the people and the traffic outside.

As Alex stepped back onto the sunny sidewalk and the door started to swing shut behind him, the old man raised the small device once more, pointed it squarely at Alex's back, and quickly pressed three buttons.

Chapter Fifteen
Hell

For a moment, the scene outside seemed exactly as he'd left it five minutes before. Smiling, well-dressed workers walked in and out of the Bright Green Mining building, which glistened in the sunshine of an almost cloudless day. Modern hydropowered cars whisked efficiently along the clean, broad, tree-lined avenue. The world, in short, looked pretty much perfect.

But only for a moment. As he stepped out of the shop and moved towards the pedestrian crossing, Alex felt a strange sensation on the back of his neck, a spark of static electricity that sent a shiver down his spine. And then, without any warning, his world changed completely.

In an instant, the color drained from the scene. People close by seemed to transform. Their clothes, which a moment before had been fashionable and colorful and new, were now tattered, torn and stained. Their formerly healthy complexions turned pallid, their bright eyes now smudged and tired. Bodies that had been well-fed and athletic shrank in on themselves and became underfed and unhealthy. The pristine street was suddenly strewn with trash. There were cracks in the sidewalk where none had been before.

The Bright Green Mining building—that shiny shrine to eco-modernity—soured into a dirty grey. The two towers behind it, formerly freshly painted in a dashing tan, metamorphosed into black, sooty smokestacks belching thick fumes. The workers spewing from the doors were dust-covered and ashen. The vehicles driving by were now ageing and rusty, their hydro-powered and electric motors transformed into gas-guzzling, polluting relics from a bygone age. The air, which had seemed so fresh and clean, now tasted acrid. All around him was a layer of smog—something he'd never encountered before. It was as if he had tumbled out of heaven and landed in hell.

Utterly disordered and disoriented, Alex stumbled backwards. Tripping on a loose, broken paving stone, he fell and landed in the gutter among broken glass, rusty cans and decaying, rotten food. He cried out as a rat ran across his foot before scampering down a storm sewer.

His mind was whirling and he felt sick. The street began swaying and spinning around him as he sat on the ground, paralyzed with fear.

A couple of people stopped and stared at him for a moment, then looked away and kept on walking. Only one person—a man standing across the street who was dressed unnervingly like the people who had taken Abby's father away—continued to watch him. The figure stepped forward as if intending to cross the road. Alex felt himself panicking, hyperventilating as the world around him came in and out of focus. He was still unable to move. He felt like he might faint.

For a moment, the sinister man across the street was hidden from view as a horde of workers from Bright Green Mining—all of whom ignored Alex—came flowing like a river from their grim workplace. As they swarmed around him, Alex felt a firm hand grip his arm, pulling him to his feet and yanking him backwards.

"This way, now!" a voice hissed urgently into his ear. Like a drowning man thrown a rope, Alex complied, letting himself be dragged away as the crowd surged around them.

A second later and the scene had vanished, the sounds of the street receding as a door closed firmly behind them. Alex heard a key turn in a lock. He turned around and saw with surprise that he was back inside the small tech shop. His savior, he realized with surprise, was the elderly, green-eyed man.

Chapter Sixteen
The Truth Unlocked

The man slid heavy bolts into place to secure the door. Next, he reached towards the window and drew down thick blinds.

Alex could not decide whether to attempt escape. Even if he tried, he was not sure he could manage it. His heart was racing and he still felt disoriented and sick to his stomach. As if reading his thoughts, the old man turned towards him and put a hand on his shoulder.

"Alex, you must calm yourself. You are safe here. I am not trying to hurt you. I'm trying to help," he said, sounding calm once more. For all his uncertainty, Alex found himself *wanting* to believe what the man said.

"Who are you?" Alex asked, still leaning against the wall as he caught his breath.

"I am John Locke, the eponymous owner of this shop. Dr. John Locke, actually. But you may call me John."

Alex paused for a moment. Dr. John Locke. The name sounded vaguely familiar, but he couldn't place it. Still, he had other things to worry about right now.

"What ... what just happened out there?" Alex asked.

"I pulled back the veil," the man answered enigmatically, still busying himself with securing the window. Alex didn't understand. He tried another tack.

"What did I just see?"

"The truth."

"That wasn't real," Alex objected instantly. "I know what the real world looks like."

"I wish that were true, Alex."

"What do you mean? Did *you* make me see those strange things?"

"Yes and no. I *allowed* you to see those things."

"How? Did you mess with my MeChip?"

"Mess with it? Not exactly. I disabled it, is all."

"Disabled it?"

"Yes. I turned off your MeChip."

"That isn't true."

"I am afraid it is. You just saw the world unfiltered. The world as it actually exists. The world *without* your MeChip."

"That doesn't make any sense," said Alex, who was starting to think more clearly now the shock of what had just happened wore off. "The MeChip's just a piece of technology to make life better, just something we use to call our friends or play games or watch shows. It can't change reality."

"It cannot change things completely, that is true, Alex. For instance, it can't change, say, a cat into a car. But it can alter your perception of reality. Consider this: the MeChip can conjure up your favorite song or book; it can diagnose an illness or phone your friends. It connects directly into your spinal cord and taps into your brain. It can make a television show appear directly in your retina, conjure a sound in your ears, even trigger scents in your olfactory senses. Is it too farfetched to think it could alter what you see, even manipulate your thoughts?"

"I guess not," Alex conceded, thinking about it. "But we know the MeChip's safe, don't we? I mean, everyone trusts Happy Corps. They're a great American company. And besides, our government wouldn't let anyone tamper with it. They would never let someone try to control the people," Alex said confidently, warming to his theme.

"But what if Happy Corp *is* the government? What if the tech titans and their political allies are feeding the American people a fake reality? What if this rose-tinted promised land you think you're in is a sham and Happy Corps is controlling your thoughts, ideas, what you see and hear? What if Americans aren't living the good life but are really slaves, overworked, underpaid, and underfed? And what if the world isn't clean and green but polluted, dirty, degraded and toxic?"

"No way! I mean, why wouldn't someone stop them? The Regs, the army, the judges, the politicians?"

"No one has stopped them Alex, because the people who really matter—the rich, the powerful—are all *part* of the conspiracy."

"Nonsense," Alex scoffed, refusing to believe it.

"Hear me out, Alex. Years ago, the elite decided it had had enough of the other 99% complaining all the time about being exploited, overworked, and underpaid. Complaints that were true, by the way. In fact, the elite were scared."

"Scared?"

"Yes, scared they might actually be forced to share all their hoarded wealth, scared they might be forced to give up a little to help make America better for everyone. This was a democracy, after all."

"It still is a democracy, Dr. Locke. Everyone knows that."

"Everyone *thinks* they know that. But it's not true. A few years before you were born, Happy Corps and the most corrupt politicians decided to do something once and for all to keep the people in line. One election night, when things were going badly for them and it looked like the people were going to elect someone who would force the billionaires to share their wealth, Happy Corp switched on the MeChip control mechanism."

"The MeChip what?"

"Control mechanism. It's a secret program installed on every MeChip."

"And what does it do?" Alex asked, his interest piqued in spite of his disbelief.

"The mechanism allows Happy Corps to alter people's perception of reality. On election night, it convinced people the elite candidate had won rather than lost. Ever since then it has been feeding the country fake images—the ones you've seen every day of your life. It has shown Americans a rose-tinted filter of the truth, shown us what we all yearn for; a better, happier, cleaner, safer world."

"But that's what we *have*," Alex insisted. "We've had it for fifteen years now. I learned about it in school."

"Ah yes. The "Great Transformation, when President Donaldson Senior managed to turn the American dream into reality," John Locke said with a smile.

"Exactly! It was a great moment in our history," Alex agreed.

"No, Alex. It was a great lie: the moment when freedom, truth and democracy were torn away from us."

Alex shook his head. How could this be true? And how did this old man know about it? Something didn't add up.

"Dr. Locke, if this is all true and we're all being brainwashed, how do you know about it?"

"That story must wait until another time," the old man answered, scratching his beard thoughtfully. "It would take too long to explain just now. And time is what we are sadly lacking."

There was another silence as Alex tried to process what he had heard. He still had difficulty believing any of it. Then another thought struck him.

"Dr. Locke, why are you telling me this?"

"I am glad you asked me that, Alex. I am telling you because I have a plan to put things right," he replied, his bright green eyes suddenly shining. "I know how to short circuit the MeChip's control mechanism. I know how to help free people—free everyone. But it won't be easy."

"So why are you telling *me*?" Alex persisted, still confused.

"Because I need you, Alex. You may not know it, but you possess a rare ability that can help free people from the MeChip's control."

"Me? What ability?"

"I cannot explain that yet. But you must know this—you are special. You can help free your fellow Americans from the curse of the MeChip. That is why I allowed you to see the truth. And now you understand, you must join me. Let me teach you the secret of how to defeat the MeChip."

Alex was silent at least a minute, thinking hard. He felt overwhelmed by this horrifying news. Was this guy crazy? And how could he, Alex, help anyway? One thing he knew for sure: he was *not* special. No, he was just an average teenager. This guy had it all wrong.

"I ... don't think so," he replied finally.

"Are you sure? Alex, you should reconsider. Believe me, the future of the country is at stake."

"But that's the problem. You see, I don't believe you. I don't believe I've been living a lie my whole life, or that the MeChip's to blame."

"Then how do you explain what you just saw outside, what you saw with Abby's father?"

"Well ... the techie at the Happy Corps shop told me someone had hacked my MeChip, not turned it off," Alex said slowly as he tried to think it through. "It must have been something you did to my MeChip. But if you are hacking it, like the techie said, it must also mean you're distorting reality, not revealing it."

"That is not the case," Dr. Locke replied firmly. "Why would I invent something like this?"

"I don't know. But you can't expect me to believe my entire existence has been a sham. And ... and I *like* my life. Or at least, I did until you got involved. If your plan is as dangerous as you say, why would I want to get involved, anyway? No, you can count me *out*. I want my old life back. And I want you to turn my MeChip back to how it was," Alex said finally, his mind made up.

"Alex, you can't mean it," the old man stated quietly and simply.

"I can and I do. I don't know what you're up to, but I want nothing to do with it. Turn my MeChip back on, Dr. Locke. Turn it on now!"

The old man stared at Alex for several seconds, as if searching for a sign he might change his mind. But Alex returned his gaze, determined to have his way.

"I said, turn it on," Alex repeated after a few seconds, his voice quiet but resolute.

The old man shook his head slowly. Reluctantly, he fished the remote out of his pocket and pressed a couple of buttons.

"Why has nothing changed?" Alex asked accusingly.

"Because my shop is the same in both worlds—just an old but tidy store."

"Will things be normal outside?"

"Yes, if you call living a lie normal," sighed the old man.

"Thank you. I'm leaving now. Please don't contact me again. I just want to return to my old life. Alright?"

"Very well, Alex. If that is what you wish. But I must warn you: there can be no safety for you, or for anyone, in that world. No matter how convincing it seems, no matter how nice it looks, the truth is the truth. And those in control are dangerous people."

"Just let me go, please," Alex said.

Sighing once more, the old man unbarred and unlocked the door.

Alex turned the handle and stepped back through the entrance without a backward glance. He just wanted to be gone from there, to be far away from this weird, unnerving old man.

Once outside, Alex looked around. With a surge of relief, he saw the sun shining as it glinted off the Bright Green Mining building, now restored to its former glory. He breathed in air that felt as fresh and clean as ever. The smog, the trash, the rats and the decay had gone. Passersby on the sidewalk looked healthy and happy once more, their tattered clothes and sunken skin now just an eerie memory. The sinister figure across the road had disappeared and the avenue looked pristine and perfect again.

Alex breathed easy.

He was back.
Back in paradise.

Chapter Seventeen
Paradise Pursued

Alex woke from a dreamless sleep. His MeChip told him it was 7:07 a.m. He leaped out of bed, tore the curtains back and looked outside.

Normal. Everything was normal. No strange hydrocars. No sinister figures in the street. No neighbors spitting blood. Nothing untoward at all. Sighing with relief, he closed the curtains and started to dress.

He had done some hard thinking the previous night. Of all the weird experiences he'd had these past few days, Alex decided, yesterday's was the weirdest. What he'd seen outside John Locke's shop had petrified him. It had seemed so real. And Locke himself had seemed so sincere, so genuine, in spite of his odd manner.

Nevertheless, Alex was certain he had been right to leave the shop, right to say no to Locke's appeal for help. The old man was clearly Crazy-Clinton. *He* might believe what he was saying, but that didn't mean Alex had to. The whole thing was too farfetched to be true.

He reflected once again on this mysterious man, Dr. John Locke. Alex felt angry the old man had messed with his MeChip. But he also felt strangely sorry for the guy. Clearly, Locke had been somebody back in the day, perhaps someone important. Now, he was obviously suffering from dementia or a mental disorder: a diminished, pathetic figure.

Alex wondered if he should try to get the old man the help he needed. Surely, there was a doctor or a clinic that could do something? After further consideration, however, Alex decided to do nothing. Things had been traumatic enough without going down the rabbit hole again to lend a hand to some eccentric old loon he knew next to nothing about. It was none of his business, he told himself firmly. Time to leave all this weird stuff behind and get back to being a normal teenager.

If he could.

His plan started well. Having made his decision, Alex had slept soundly that night for the first time in almost a week. His morning had started normally, too. Could it last?

He arrived at school about ten minutes before his first lesson. The classroom was empty except for Sol and Tom, who were already in their usual places near the back. They were talking animatedly, their heads close together. As Alex walked in, they looked up and Tom whispered something to Sol, who nodded. What were they talking about, Alex wondered? It didn't take long for him to find out.

"Hey, Alex. How are you?" Sol asked, a guarded expression on his face.

"I'm fine."

"Really?"

"Yes, really. Why?"

"Well, because, you know ..." he trailed off, looking at Tom for support. His friend sighed and took up the thread.

"What Sol's trying to say is, you've been weird lately. And I don't mean your usual awkward dexter self, but really, really weird."

"Nice one, Tom. Way to hit the subtle button," Sol interrupted. "Seriously, for you to call anyone a dexter is all sorts of wrong. You're the dexter king, Thomas. Maybe even the emperor, who knows? But yeah, Alex, we're worried about you. Are you okay?" he asked, his forehead creasing with concern.

"Guys, I'm fine," Alex replied, forcing a smile.

"Really? Cause you don't seem fine," Sol said, still frowning.

"Okay, I'm not fine. Some weird things have happened lately. Really weird," Alex confessed.

"Want to talk about it?" Tom asked.

"I wouldn't know where to start," Alex admitted. "Look, I know I've been a bit off-grid lately, but from now on I'm determined to get back on track. Life's going to go back to how it was before."

"Okay ..." Sol sounded doubtful.

"Are you sure you don't want to tell us what's going on?" Tom asked again, at the same time lowering his voice as other students began to drift into the room and take their seats.

"No," Alex said quietly after pausing to think about it for a moment. "I just want to put it all behind me, try to forget about it and move forward. Is that okay?"

"It's fine with us," Sol said, looking from Alex to Tom, who nodded his agreement.

"And that includes getting back on track with our music, right?" Sol prompted.

"Yes," Alex agreed. "No more faffing about. I'll talk to my mom again, see if I can convince her to let us practice after school. We've still got two weeks to nail this before the competition."

"Sounds good, Alex," Tom said, smiling as he clapped his friend on the back.

"Should we rehearse at lunchtime, too?" Sol asked as the teacher walked into the room.

"Maybe tomorrow," Alex replied. "Today, there's someone I really need to talk to."

Chapter Eighteen
Mom and Mr. X

The corridor was crowded with kids heading to the cafeteria or the courtyard as Alex left his friends and made his way against the tide of people and towards another classroom. He arrived just as a bunch of students from the year below filed out of the room. It sounded like the lesson had been fun, for Alex overheard snippets of animated conversation as the fourteen-year-olds left for lunch.

"Nice job on the synthi-drum ..."

"... didn't know I could play like that ..."

"... Mrs. Franklin's the best ..."

"... wish they were all like her ..."

Alex felt a small glow of pride as the last teenager left the room and he entered. The music class was filled with instruments, while the mannequin Mr. X was in his usual spot, his ancient X-shaped guitar still strapped across his shoulders. Alex barely noticed any of this, though, for his attention was all on his mom. She was sitting quite still behind her desk. From her silence, Alex guessed she was checking her MeChip for messages.

"Hey Mom, it's me," he said quietly.

She looked up, moving her lips as she spoke quietly to herself. Alex always found it amusing when older people spoke to their MeChips. They knew—as everyone did—that they could just instruct it using their thoughts. Yet so many old people seemed to feel the need to talk to their MeChips. He wondered idly if it was because older people hadn't grown up with them? But his mind was wandering, he realized, and with an effort he brought it back to the present, where his mom was looking at him expectantly.

"Yes, Alex?"

"Those kids liked your lesson," he said, nodding towards the exit.

"Really?" his mom asked. "How do you know?"

"I just heard them talking about it as they left the room. They think you're great!"

"Oh, that's lovely," she said, her face brightening. "I'm glad I can share my passion for music with them," she added. "Was that what you came to tell me?"

"No," Alex admitted. "Do you have a millisec to talk about something else, something important?"

"Of course. What's up?"

"Listen, Mom, I just wanted to say I'm sorry if I've seemed ... off, lately. There've been a few weird things going on that threw me for a loop."

"Thank you for saying sorry, Alex. That means a lot to me. Now, would you like to talk about it ...about what's been going on, I mean?" she said, looking at her son with concern.

"I don't think so," he replied after a pause, again feeling that odd reluctance to relive what had happened, that hesitation about sharing his troubles even with those closest to him. "I think I just want to put it behind me. Get back to normal and keep my head down for a while. Is that okay?

"Yes, it's okay, Alex," she said slowly. "But you know I'm always here for you. Your dad, too. Right?"

"I know. Thanks, Mom."

"So how's band practice going?" she asked, changing the subject. "Can you at least talk about that?" she added, smiling once more.

"Sure. That's a whole other problem," he admitted.

"What do you mean?"

"Remember what happened last year in the Best Band contest when I ... well, when I froze onstage? It was humiliating."

"I know it was, Alex. But that was a year ago. You've come a long way with your playing since then," his mother said, trying to reassure him.

"I guess," he answered.

"So, Alex, what's really worrying you?"

He was silent for a moment before, finally, all of his worries came tumbling out:

"The thing is some of the kids here just won't let me forget about it, especially Iggy, and the other day he challenged me to a guitar playoff in this room and although I didn't freeze exactly, I did panic, and he beat me in front of a whole bunch of kids. And he's such a good guitarist. Everyone says it, even you. And I'm just afraid that even though I love music and playing guitar when I'm by myself, or with Sol and Tom, I can't do anything right in public, and I'll mess up again at the Best Band contest in front of the whole school and Iggy will win hands down again and, honestly Mom, I'm just really terrified!" he said, the words gushing out in a torrent, like water bursting through a crumbling dam.

His mom looked at him for several seconds, her head tilted to one side in that way Alex knew signaled she was worried and thinking hard.

"Alex, I know you're anxious about the competition. And you're right that I praise Iggy sometimes—"

"You see! Even you think he'll win," Alex interrupted.

"That's not true," Mrs. Franklin replied firmly, holding her hand up to stop him. "I praise him because he's a good musician. And he is. But so are you, Alex. I'm sorry if I haven't told you that enough. Perhaps I'm tougher on you because I see your potential and I want you to reach it. I know if you keep working hard and just believe in yourself a little bit more you can be a great musician."

"Good enough to win the Best Band contest?"

"Definitely!" his mother said, her smile broadening.

"But what about Iggy? He's good too. And he's got something I don't have anymore ..."

"What's that, Alex?"

"Confidence," Alex said quietly, dropping his eyes and staring at the ground.

"Alex, have you ever wondered why Iggy is so competitive with you, why he keeps trying to put you down?"

"Because he's better than me?" Alex asked.

"No, Alex. Quite the opposite, in fact. He singles you out over every other musician in the school because he knows you're the one person who could beat him. He sees your potential, Alex. Why else do you think he'd even bother with you, if you weren't a threat to his crown?"

"But he just beat me again the other day."

"Yes, but I heard you ran him close. Oh, I know all about it already—you don't think I'd miss news like that, do you?' she said, smiling again. "Perhaps he thinks if he can keep you feeling insecure and inferior, he can keep winning."

"He humiliated me, Mom. I couldn't remember the notes. I was like a statue, like ... like ... well, like Mr. X here," he said, looking at the mannequin on the wall.

"Hey, there's nothing wrong with old Mr. X!" his mom laughed. "I'll bet he was a great musician in his day. In fact, I bet Mr. X is like me—we've still got it when we need it! Listen."

His mom stood up and walked towards the synthi-piano in the corner of the room. Sitting down, she started playing an old tune from the Retro-Before Time, light and uplifting. The mood and the tempo were inspiring, infectious.

"Wow, Mom, you still got it!" Alex enthused when she finished. "That was smeckin' great! Why don't you play anymore? I haven't heard you in ages."

"I still practice every day, Alex, using my headset or MeChip. I just play for myself since your father gave up guitar, that's all. And practice is what it comes down to in the end. Plenty of practice and a pinch of self-belief.

"If I can play guitar someday as well as you play piano, I'll be happy."

"You're closer than you think, Alex. Like mother like son, right? Just keep working at it and start believing in yourself."

"Thanks, Mom. I will. Speaking of practicing, I don't suppose you would—"

"Let you off being grounded so you can practice after school?" she cut in, reading his thoughts.

"Yeah. Would that be okay? Pretty please!"

"Alright," she said, shaking her head and smiling to herself. "But you need to apologize to Abby and her father for that incident the other day, okay?"

"Okay," Alex nodded. "Thanks, Mom!" he said, leaning in to kiss her on the cheek before turning to leave.

Alex felt elated as he departed the music room. Now they could start rehearsing daily after school, although speaking to Abby and her dad felt like a steep price to pay. That would be *uber* awkward, he realized.

He was trying to figure out how he might get out of this embarrassing task—or at least postpone it for a while—when he turned a corner and collided with Abby herself, accidentally scattering her pile of books and papers across the corridor.

"Hey, why don't you watch where you're ... oh, it's you," she said, as she saw who'd done it.

"Oh, smeck! Here, let me help," he said as he bent down next to her and started gathering up her stuff. "Sorry about that. I didn't mean to scare you or make this mess. Are you okay?" he asked anxiously.

"Yeah, I'm fine. But what about you? Are you okay, Alex?"

"What do you ... oh, that. Yeah, I'm alright, I think. But listen, I'm sorry about the other day. I just got confused, I guess. Things have been really difficult lately. It's hard to explain. The main thing is I'm back on track and won't be making any trouble from now on. I'll leave you and Iggy in peace. Okay?"

"Sure. Yes. That's good. Listen, take care of yourself, Alex, okay?" she said, looking at him earnestly for a moment.

"I will. Thanks, Abby. And ... sorry."

For a moment she looked like she wanted to say something else. As she stood looking at him, an unexpected wave of nostalgia flooded into Alex's mind: memories of their shared friendship from years before, times spent playing in their gardens and having adventures on their bikes as kids.

Abby opened her mouth, closed it, bit her lip and ran a hand through her lustrous brown hair, still looking at him with a curious expression. He waited for her to speak, curious if she too was remembering their earlier closeness, desperate to know what she might have to say to him. Whatever she was thinking, though, was never shared. At that moment, two students rounded the corner and the spell was broken. Abby turned away and walked suddenly down the corridor without a backwards glance.

Chapter Nineteen
Paradise Found

Drums rapped out a percussive beat as the bass guitar pulsed rhythmically. Alex's voice soared above them, finally trailing away as Tom crashed down twice more with his sticks to bring the song to a powerful close. The garage fell silent. The three friends looked at one another, each awaiting a reaction. After several seconds, Sol started nodding slowly while Tom broke into a broad grin, reaching out to high-five his bandmates.

"Nice. Smeckin' nice! Alex, when you said you were going to get back on the straight and narrow you really meant it. This has been the best two weeks ever. We've come a long way, gentlemen, and we're sounding sweet!" Tom declared ecstatically.

"I have to agree. Even you were pretty decent tonight, Tom," Sol said seriously.

"I'll take that as a compliment coming from you, my grumpy little friend. You're almost smiling. It's a miracle," Tom teased.

"We were good though, weren't we?" Alex said, still thinking about their performance.

"Good? No, Alex. We were great! And you, my friend, are on fire right now," Tom replied confidently. "Maybe we can even win the nationals this time. I know Iggy did well in the regionals last year but no one from here has ever taken the ultimate prize before. Maybe we can one-up him?"

"Let's not get ahead of ourselves, Tom. We have to beat Iggy in the locals first and that's not going to be easy, even if we're at our best," Sol said soberly.

"Oh, there's the little pessimist I know and loathe!" Tom said. "Listen to me, Sunshine Sol, I'm not saying we *will* win, I'm just saying we *could*."

"I guess we'll find out one way or the other tomorrow night. I can't believe it's so soon," Alex said.

"I hear you on that," Sol agreed.

"I wonder how Iggy's rehearsals have been going? I think they've stopped practicing in school. Have you heard anything?" Alex asked the others.

"Nothing at all," admitted Tom, who usually had all the gossip. "I think they're preparing somewhere, but totally on the downlow. Still, they can't have improved as much as we have. No way. Man, the ladies are just gonna love us," Tom said enthusiastically.

"I don't know. Say what you like about Iggy, but he trains hard. I hope they don't have something up their sleeve," Alex persisted.

"Quit worrying, you dexter. Listen, you can't think about him now. Just stick to our game plan. Let's run through the song one more time, okay?" Tom said, as the three friends took up their instruments again.

Tom was right, Alex thought happily as he headed home from rehearsal fifteen minutes later. It had been a good couple of weeks. Great, even.

First, their rehearsals had gone superbly and the band were at their best level yet. Each of them had been practicing by themselves every morning before school, as well as spending hours training together each evening. They were getting tighter and tighter.

Secondly, and more importantly for Alex's sanity, nothing weird had happened. No sick neighbors, no sinister strangers, no unnerving visions of a darker, more disturbing world, and no messages from that elderly oddball, Dr. Locke. In fact, life had been so normal, and so much better, the events of a few weeks before seemed almost like a dream.

Not that things were perfect. There was still the small issue of Iggy and Abby being an item. And Alex still had an odd sensation whenever he saw Abby's dad, even if he had persuaded himself it must just have been his imagination that the man was a little different these days. Alex was also nervous—very nervous—about tomorrow night's Best Band contest. While he knew he couldn't have done more or worked harder to prepare, the thought of going onto the stage in front of all those people still gave him the jeepsters.

Still, he thought as he unlocked his front door and stepped inside the house, things had turned out a lot better than he'd feared.

"Alex, is that you?" came his mom's voice from the kitchen.

"Who else?" he smiled as he entered the room.

"It's after eight. You must be starving. Dinner's in the oven," she said as Alex went to fetch his food.

"How was practice?" she asked as he sat down to eat.

"Great. Really great. You know, I'm starting to think we have a chance tomorrow after all."

"Of course you do! You've practiced so hard. If you do win, you'll deserve it," she said, beaming at him.

"Your mom's right. We're proud of you whatever happens, son. You've really turned things around these past couple of weeks," his dad chimed in.

"Thanks, guys. I must admit, it feels like I've put my problems behind me now. That week when things went weird already feels like a bad dream."

"Let's hope so. We don't want them coming back, do we?" his dad replied, winking conspiratorially at his son.

Alex had just finished his nachos when there was a sharp knock at the door.

"Are you expecting anyone, Alex?" his mom asked, eyebrows raised.

"No. How about you, Dad?"

But his father seemed as surprised as he was.

"Let me get it," Alex said, jumping up. "I'm done with dinner anyway." Before either parent could move, their son had stepped out into the hallway and was walking briskly towards the front door. He was still thinking about how well things were going, his mind only half on the task at hand, when he reached the handle and pulled it open.

Instantly, his smile vanished and a sensation of sickness surged through his stomach. He could barely believe it, barely believe who was standing there on the doorstep, like a nightmare come to life.

It was Locke.

Dr. John Locke.

And he had a look of terror on his face.

Chapter Twenty
Paradise Lost

The elderly man was leaning against the door frame and breathing hard. His green eyes were narrowed as he looked at Alex. He glanced to left and right, then over his shoulder. Alex noticed he was wearing the same vintage-style clothes as before: collared shirt, tie, dark pants, patented leather shoes. His lined forehead glistened with sweat.

"We don't have much time. They know," he said simply, still gasping as if he'd run here all the way from his shop.

"Dr. Locke. What are you doing here? I thought I told you to stay away," Alex said, his anger rising at the presence of this unwelcome intruder.

"It's too late for that. Did you hear what I just said, Alex? They know."

"Know what?" Alex said, his curiosity getting the better of him in spite of his fear and irritation.

"About you, of course. I can't protect you anymore. Not here, at least. You have to escape. Come with me now," Dr. Locke said, his voice shaking slightly with obvious agitation.

"No. Why? I don't want to escape. This is ridiculous."

"You don't have a choice, Alex. They're coming," he said, glancing at a vintage watch on his wrist.

"Nonsense. You should leave," Alex said, starting to close the door on this uninvited interloper.

"They'll be here in two minutes," Dr. Locke replied as, with a rapidity that belied his age, he moved his foot forward to prevent the door closing.

“I don’t believe you. I’m getting my parents.”

“Your parents can’t help you, Alex. If I’m right they’ll have been turned off. It always happens exactly two minutes before a snatch.”

Alex stared at him in confusion.

“What did you just say?”

“I said your parents will have been turned off. They’ll have used the MeChip control mechanism by now.”

Alex stared at him dumbly. That couldn’t be true. Could it?

“Go check if you don’t believe me,” Dr. Locke said, as if reading Alex’s mind. “But hurry.”

Alex turned and ran back to the kitchen. His parents were seated exactly where he’d left them. He breathed a sigh of relief. He’d been right. The old man was crazy ... deranged.

“Mom, Dad, there’s a weird old man at the door. Can you help me get rid of him?” he asked.

They didn’t answer. Their heads were bowed a little, their eyes half closed. Alex’s heart began to hammer.

“Mom? Dad?” he asked again.

Nothing.

He went up to them, put his hand on his mom’s shoulder. No response. In desperation, he waved a hand in front of his dad’s eyes, tried to shake him from his torpor.

Still nothing. His dad rocked slightly with the motion of Alex’s pushing and pulling, but he did not register his son’s presence. It was as if he were frozen.

Panicking, Alex ran back to the door. The old man was waiting patiently; he seemed calmer now and was breathing more easily.

Alex grabbed Dr. Locke by the front of his shirt with one hand, pulling his other arm back and balling his fingers into a fist, ready to punch him.

“What’s wrong with them? What the smeck have you done!?” he said, as fury and fear fought for the upper hand.

"Nothing. I promise you it isn't me," Dr. Locke insisted, his eyes never leaving Alex's. "I'm trying to tell you, Alex, they're coming. We have sixty seconds to get out. Please let me in. I'm begging you," he said, a touch of his earlier desperation creeping back into his voice.

Alex hesitated, unsure what to do. Part of him still wanted to believe Locke was behind this, that he was messing with people's MeChips again. It would be so much easier, so much *better*, if it was just one crazy old man making mischief. But there was something in the man's eyes, something that told Alex that Locke was sincere. With a sigh, Alex stepped aside and let the man in the house.

Instantly, Locke slammed the door behind him and locked it.

"Thank you, Alex. Thank you for trusting me. Now, is there another way out? A back door? We must leave."

"What about my parents? Can you wake them?"

"No, Alex. They will be fine. The best thing you can do is leave them here. It's not your parents they're after, it's you. Somehow, they've found out you're a threat."

"Me? But I'm not a threat to anyone. And I can't leave Mom and Dad here like this. Not if what you said is true."

"They'll be safer here, Alex. It's you they want," Locke insisted. "Alex, if we don't leave now they're going to snatch you and reprocess you," he added, looking once again at his antique watch.

"What do you mean?"

"No time to explain."

"I'm not going anywhere until you do," Alex said fiercely, crossing his arms.

"Oh, very well," Locke said, speaking rapidly as if every second counted. "They're coming here to replace you, just like they did with Abby's father. But in your case they're going to reprocess you—lobotomize you by removing a part of your brain to make you safe and harmless. Then, assuming you survive, they will place you with another family."

"You can't be serious!" Alex said, shocked.

"Deadly. Oh no, they're here!"

Alex heard the sound of a car pulling up outside. Standing on his toes, he looked through the glass panel at the top of the front door. A black vehicle similar to the one he'd seen the night Abby's father was taken had just pulled up directly outside their house. As Alex watched in horror, four figures in long, dark coats climbed out and started walking purposefully towards his front door. Behind them, Alex caught sight of another figure, shorter, slimmer. With a shock, he realized the figure was dressed like a teenager, was in fact a young man who bore more than a passing resemblance to ... him!

At the same time, there came the sound of chairs scraping on the floor in the kitchen, as if being pushed back. His parents entered the hallway, heads still bowed as they shuffled slowly, zombie-like, towards the front door.

"Dr. Locke, you have to stop them! We have to save my parents. We have to *fight*," Alex insisted.

"We can't. Not here. Not yet. Alex, listen to me. I can teach you how to stop this—how to fight back—but right now we need to escape. It's the only way we can save your parents, or Abby."

"Abby?"

"I'll explain later. Come on, or it really will be too late!"

Reluctantly Alex led Locke past his parents, who were now almost at the front door.

They entered the kitchen just as Alex heard the sound of the front door being unlocked. Evidently, his parents were opening it to these intruders, just as Abby's mom had let them into her home a few weeks earlier.

"Follow me," Alex said, leading the old man through the kitchen and down a second corridor towards a rear door. Moving as quickly as he could, Alex unlocked the door, trying to ignore the sounds of footsteps coming from inside the house. Urgently, he tugged it open ...

and cursed to himself as it creaked loudly on its hinges. He'd promised his dad that he'd oil them only last weekend, but had somehow forgotten. If only he'd done this one chore! Now, it could be the difference between freedom and capture.

The sound of footsteps stopped for a moment as the hinges squealed, then became louder as they followed the direction of the sound. A second later, Alex saw the figures emerge from the kitchen into the rear corridor, spot them, and hasten forward.

Locke and Alex dashed out into the back garden and ran towards the neighbors' fence. Faster than the old man, Alex reached it first and vaulted over, then stopped to help his comrade. In spite of his advanced years, Locke was agile and athletic, Alex saw, stopping only to put one foot on top of the railing before leaping lightly onto the other side.

"This way," he grunted as he led Alex towards the front of the neighbors' garden, the sinister figures no more than twenty paces behind.

Locke and Alex fled up the neighbor's front path, pushed open the small gate, and dashed towards the far end of the street. Alex saw Locke point a small device ahead of him, heard it beep as he pressed it. In answer, a hydrocar not thirty steps ahead of them lit up, its doors opening automatically.

"It's mine! Come on," Locke urged as they sprinted forward.

Alex never saw the tree root in the darkness. It caught his toe and he fell heavily, sprawling onto the sidewalk, grazing shins and palms. Instantly he tried to get back to his feet and run to the hydrocar—too late.

A hand grabbed his wrist, holding him firmly as he tried to pull away. Then a second figure reached him, restraining him by his other arm. A third individual was approaching fast, just a few steps behind. Alex tugged and strained desperately, but it was no use. The men were far too strong. He cried out in fear and alarm and saw Locke, who was twenty yards ahead and about to reach the car, look up, surprise registering on his face.

"We have him. We have the boy," one of the figures said in a flat, unemotional monotone to his MeChip as Alex continued to struggle frantically to escape. But it was futile, he knew. He could not get away. He was trapped.

Or was he? Suddenly the grip of the two men loosened. As he looked at them, he was surprised to see both lapse into the same semi-conscious state as his parents, their heads now bowed, jaws slack, arms hanging limply by their sides as they stood there, silent and unmoving. Looking ahead, he saw Locke holding the same remote control he'd had in the shop. It was pointed at the two men. The third man brushed past Alex and rushed at Locke, but a press of a button immobilized him, too.

Alex ran forward towards the hydrocar and safety. Locke and Alex were about to clamber into the vehicle when they heard a voice from behind.

"Reboot!"

Alex saw the three frozen figures begin slowly to move, lifting their heads groggily and looking around uncertainly as if awaking from a long sleep. One of them fell stiffly to his knees, then slowly began to raise himself once more.

Meanwhile, another man emerged from the shadows. He walked purposefully towards the car, stopping just fifteen paces away. Alex saw a stocky, powerfully-built, middle-aged man in a dark greatcoat. His hair was cut short, brown but flecked with grey. His face was stern as he peered at them from hooded blue eyes.

"John Locke! I should have known you would do something like this eventually," the man said in a deep, commanding voice that sounded accustomed to giving orders and having them obeyed. "You're much too old for such foolishness, Locke. Give up the boy and I can make it easy for you. Don't make me chainstitch you, John."

"Slade Arnold," Locke said simply. He met the man's gaze for just a moment before turning to look once again at Alex. Motioning for him to get into the car, he climbed inside. Alex was about to join him when the strange man spoke again.

"Alexander Franklin ... Alex. Do not get in the car. Give yourself up to me. It will be better for you, much better. Trust me," he said, his voice deep and so quiet Alex had to strain to hear him.

Something about the man's tone stopped Alex in his tracks and for a moment he almost obeyed.

Only for a moment. As one of the man's companions started to regain his self-control and lurched forward, Alex snapped out of his frozen state and quickly jumped inside the vehicle, shutting the door behind him. Instantly, Locke started the engine. Without another word, he engaged the gears and pulled away, accelerating rapidly.

In his side mirror, Alex saw the man still standing on the sidewalk, his eyes fixed on their quickly retreating car. He was shaking his head slightly, his arms folded across his broad chest. The last thing Alex saw as they turned a corner and drove away were the three other figures, still moving slowly but clearly in control of themselves once more as they gathered around their forbidding leader.

Chapter Twenty-One
Hot Chocolate

They drove in silence for several minutes. Locke seemed singularly focused on steering and Alex felt too shocked, too numb, to speak. The roads were quiet, with only a few vehicles coming and going in the darkness. There was no sign of pursuit.

They were just passing Alex's school when Locke slowed his car and pulled over. He drew the weird remote from his pocket once more, then looked at his passenger.

"I'm going to disable your MeChip," Locke said simply.

"Why?" Alex asked, surprised.

"So they can't track us. But I must warn you: it will show you the world without the MeChip filter, like what you saw outside my shop. Are you ready for this?"

"Not really," Alex answered honestly. "But go ahead," he added, bracing himself.

Locke pressed several buttons in quick succession. Alex felt a sudden jolt at the back of his neck, like a mild electric shock. He shut his eyes involuntarily, then opened them slowly.

It was back. There could be no doubt about it. Even with his vision limited by the darkness of the evening, his world had changed. The car interior looked shabbier, its previously pristine digital display of flashing lights now morphing into an old-school, cracked speedometer. The seats were no longer plush leather but a worn-out nylon fabric, fraying in parts. As he shifted his gaze to look through the windshield, he saw his school was not fronted by shining chrome and steel but some inferior metal, rusting badly in parts. The glass windows were dirty and one or two looked broken. The flagpole, where their country's standard with its stars and stripes was proudly hauled up each morning, was peeling and chipped. The whole scene was clouded by something Alex thought at first was fog, then realized must be a dirty smog. His mind flashed back to what had just happened at the house, to those terrifying intruders and his parents' zombie-like state.

So it was real, then, Alex admitted to himself. Everything Locke had said was real. There could be no more doubting, now. This, he realized, was the final proof.

"Are you alright?" Locke asked, his forehead creased with concern.

"I guess," Alex whispered.

Locke looked at him for another moment before turning the key in the ignition, starting the engine, and driving once more into the night. Neither of them spoke for several minutes.

"Dr. Locke. Where are we going?" Alex asked eventually, his curiosity finally getting the better of his fears.

"Eh? What's that?" Locke replied, evidently lost in thoughts of his own.

"Are we going to your shop, sir?"

"No, they could be there already. We're going someplace else. Someplace safe. And do, please, call me John."

"Where are we going, then ... John?"

"Best for you not to know."

"Is it far?"

"No, not far. It's here in town. We'll be there in a few minutes."

"Dr. Locke, who was that man?" Alex asked, forgetting once more to use his first name.

"All in good time, Alex. Let us get to our destination first."

They drove through streets Alex knew well, although even in the dimness of a moonless night he saw with a sinking feeling that they looked more run down than before. The cars in the driveways were older, the houses more neglected, the picket fences peeling and broken in places, and the trees that lined the blocks sickly and stunted. Everywhere was that haze of pollution. This smog, this contamination, was something he'd read about in books, something that had apparently existed before the Great Transformation many years before. It was not supposed to exist today. The teachers had told him it had been solved during President Donaldson Senior's second term in office. Now he knew that was a lie. How could it be real when the evidence was all around him?

Soon, Locke was driving through parts of their small city Alex didn't recognize. Some of these seemed in an even worse state than his own neighborhood, with trash on the streets and signs everywhere of disrepair and decay. Streetlamps flickered or were not working at all. Houses and apartment blocks were dilapidated and, in some cases, looked abandoned. Their drive became bumpier as Locke's car crossed deep potholes or cracks in the concrete. Finally, Locke turned down a side street and pulled into a driveway, halting in front of an old garage. The elderly man pressed a button by the steering wheel and the garage door automatically lifted. He eased the vehicle forward, then pressed the button again, shutting them inside.

They got out of the car and Locke led them through an interior entryway into a room. He flipped a switch on the wall and a soft light came on. They were in a kitchen. It looked small but homey, and for a moment Alex thought his MeChip must be working again. Then he noticed the appliances: a spotless but ancient General Electric gas stove top, an antique Kenmore fridge, and a stainless-steel sink, bright and shiny but seeming from its shape and design to come from another age, perhaps even another century. All were pleasant enough and marked a reassuring contrast to the dirt and grime outside. Yet all were too antiquated, too outdated for his former MeChip-controlled world.

Thinking back, he could only ever recall the MeChip presenting him with the modern, the futuristic. Except perhaps for the occasional visit to a museum or the odd retro television show he'd seen on his

MeChip, he could recall nothing like this. Even these old memories seemed hazy, somehow. Had they, too, been tampered with, he wondered?

Alex looked up from the appliances and saw rows of old cabinets on the walls painted in a jaunty teal color that had never been in fashion during his lifetime. Faded, flower-patterned curtains concealed a narrow window. A small, round wooden table with four chairs sat squarely in the middle of the room. With the wave of his hand, Locke motioned for Alex to sit down.

As he did so, Alex noticed a very thin film of dust, which made him think the house was not in regular use, although it was otherwise clean enough. Meanwhile, Locke was busying himself, lighting one of the gas hobs, pulling out a small kettle from a shelf, filling it with water, and beginning to heat the liquid on the stove top. Locke then pulled two plastic containers from a drawer, as well as two ceramic mugs.

Alex watched his host with only the vaguest interest. Now they were out of any imminent danger, he felt drained and tired. For a moment he laid his head on the table, then lifted it again as Locke placed something next to him.

"What's this?"

"Hot chocolate," Locke said with a small smile.

Alex sat up and tasted the drink, swallowing a mouthful. As the warm, sweet fluid flowed into him, he relaxed and sighed out loud.

Locke took the seat next to his, watching him for a moment. The elderly man reached into his pocket and pulled out a silver flask, pouring some amber liquid into his own hot drink. Alex caught just a whiff of something aromatic and spicy, pungent but not unpleasant.

"Just a little something extra for mine. Purely medicinal, you understand," Locke said, his green eyes twinkling mischievously in a way Alex hadn't seen before.

Alex smiled back and let out a long yawn, covering his mouth belatedly in case it seemed rude.

"Sorry," he muttered.

"No need to apologize, Alex. You must be absolutely spent."

"I guess," Alex replied. "But ... we should talk," he continued, yawning again in spite of himself. "There's so much I want to ask you, so much I need to know."

"We will talk, Alex," Locke agreed. "But not yet. First, I can see you need to sleep. You have had quite an adventure and several shocks to the system. Before we do anything else, you must rest. Things will make more sense then."

"But—"

"No, Alex. Rest first, talk later. Come on, let me show you to your room."

Alex drained the last of his hot chocolate before following his host, who led him into another room and then down a short corridor with two doorways on either side. The man pointed ahead to the last room on the right.

"You can sleep in there. It's nothing much, I'm afraid. Just a small bed and a dresser. The light switch is just inside the door on the right. The bathroom is through the door opposite."

"But—"

"Goodnight, Alex," Locke said gently but firmly as he turned and walked back in the direction of the kitchen.

With a third yawn, this one the longest of all, Alex decided Locke was right. There was so much he had to think about, so much he wanted to know. But not now. For now, what he needed, what he desperately needed, was to rest. In welcome silence, he made his way sleepily down the corridor. Tomorrow, he told himself as his head hit the pillow, he would get all the answers he needed.

Chapter Twenty-Two
The Test

Alex awoke in sunlight as a thin band of brightness penetrated a gap in the curtains and pierced his consciousness. He had slept soundly and dreamlessly all night, but now his brain felt foggy and unclear, still halfway between slumber and wakefulness. He sat up, unsure for a moment where he was. He tried to check the time on his MeChip, but it didn't respond.

"Mom? Dad? Where are you?!" he called out, his heart beginning to race as his mind tried to put back in place the pieces of the previous night.

"Alex, it's me, John. You're not at home. You're here at the safe house, remember?" the old man said reassuringly as he appeared at the bedroom door. Locke's sudden presence triggered a rush of recollections on Alex's part. The boy inhaled deeply in an effort to calm himself, then nodded.

"I'll let you wake up properly. Breakfast will be ready in fifteen minutes," Locke said, looking at him for a moment before leaving him alone once more.

Alex took several deep breaths to steady himself, got up and used the bathroom. So, it hadn't all been a dream, then. He was here, in this new world. Or more accurately, this *old* world. He washed his face in cold water, cleaned his teeth using a toothbrush left for him by the sink and still in its packaging, dressed and emerged into the kitchen a few minutes later, now fully awake and determined to face the truth.

"What time is it?" he asked as he entered. Locke looked up from a frying pan as he busied himself with breakfast.

"It is 9:07," he muttered, briefly scanning his watch before returning to his task.

"What's cooking?" Alex asked as he breathed in an alluring array of odors.

"Fried eggs, hash browns, toast, coffee. I do hope you're hungry," the old man said, smiling to himself without looking up.

"Definitely!" Alex grinned. "Can I help?"

"No, but thank you for asking, Alex. I can tell your parents brought you up right. Take a seat. It's almost ready."

The food was delicious. Between that and the long, uninterrupted sleep, it was quite a different Alex who pushed his seat back, satisfied after this filling meal, and rose to take his dirty plate to the sink. The two of them worked in silence for several minutes, washing and drying the dishes. Finally, Locke filled their coffee cups again and motioned for Alex to sit down.

"So, Alex, let's talk. What do you wish to know first?"

"My parents—are they okay?" Alex began.

"For the time being, yes. As I said last night, they were not the target of the Fixers. You were."

"So Mom and Dad will be back at home still?"

"I believe so, yes," Locke nodded.

"And they'll be back to normal? Their MeChips back on, I mean?"

Again, Locke nodded.

"But won't they notice I'm gone?"

"No."

"Why not?" Alex asked, although he had already guessed the answer.

"Because as far as they are concerned, you are *not* gone. By now you will probably have been replaced by that other boy, the teenager who looked a little like you, the one who was brought by the Fixers."

Alex couldn't speak for a moment. Could he really be replaced so easily? He frowned to himself, trying to frame his next question while

Locke sipped on his coffee looking expectantly at the young man sitting across the table from him.

"Wouldn't my parents know? I mean, surely they'd see that boy isn't me?" Alex asked.

"No. They will think it is you because their MeChips will tell them so."

"But I'm their son! How could they not recognize their own son?" Alex exclaimed, his voice rising with angst and uncertainty.

"The MeChip's programming is very strong and continues to be improved with each passing year. Trust me, Alex. They will think it is you; a fact that should, incidentally, keep them safe."

Alex was silent again. In spite of himself, he felt angry at his parents. *Don't they love me enough to know who I am?*

"Alex, your parents care about you very much," Locke said, as if reading his thoughts. "But the MeChip is more dominant than you imagine. Recall, it sits in your spinal cord, can feed sensations, sights, sounds, smells, even ideas directly into your brain. It is hard to resist its effects, especially if you do not even know what it is really doing."

Alex still couldn't bring himself to speak and after a few moments, Locke continued.

"If it is any consolation, Alex, I am convinced your parents do sense this boy is not you. A parent's love is strong. Deep down in their subconscious minds, they will know the truth. They may feel confusion or uncertainty, a vague sense something is amiss. Of course, the MeChip will suppress their knowledge of what, exactly, is wrong. But their feelings for you have not gone away, just been obscured and redirected. The MeChip has many strengths, but it cannot fully eradicate that type of love."

"You're saying it has weaknesses, then?"

"Two that I know of, Alex. Would you like me to show you one?"

Alex nodded, eager to find a way to fight back.

"Wait here, Alex," Locke said, standing up and heading towards the garage.

As Alex sat sipping his coffee and reflecting on what he'd just learned, he felt an unexpected emotion.

Hate.

He was starting to hate the MeChip now. He'd always liked it in the past, taken it for granted as something that was benign, something that made his life easier and more fun. Now he felt only anger and disgust. He despised this thing, this technology, not only for forcing him to live a lie his entire life, but for fooling his parents into taking another child, a cuckoo, into their home. How could anyone misuse something like this, he wondered? The MeChip should be a force for good.

Alex's dark thoughts were interrupted as Locke re-entered the room. He was carrying something behind his back which he placed on the ground by the table, just out of sight.

"Alex, to do this ... um ... experiment, I will need to turn your MeChip back on. Don't worry, I'll only re-engage its sensory filters. It won't make you traceable again. We'll be quite safe here," Locke assured him as he pulled out his remote once more, this time pressing at least half-a-dozen buttons one after the next in a complex sequence.

As he pressed the final button, Alex felt that now-familiar jolt of electricity at the back of his neck. Again, he shut his eyes involuntarily, then opened them warily.

It was as if the sun had come out from behind grey, brooding clouds. One moment, the room was dark, with pale light filtering through the curtains on the old appliances and linoleum floor. The next, the room was shiny and bright, the appliances new and modern, the curtains sporting the latest patterns and colors. Even the table looked freshly polished. In spite of himself, Alex had to admit; the MeChip's artificial world was definitely easy on the eyes.

"Is it working?" Locke asked. Alex nodded. The old man leaned down, picked the object he'd brought in from the garage off the floor and placed it on the table.

"What do you see?"

"Flowers," Alex answered instantly.

"Anything else?"

"Well, they're in a vase," Alex explained.

"Good. And how do they look?"

"Umm ... nice, I guess."

"And their color is ...?"

"Yellow, mostly. A few are purple."

"How do they smell?"

"Nice. Fresh," Alex replied, breathing in through his nose while at the same time feeling a little confused. What was this all about, he wondered?

"Alright. Now, Alex, I want you to focus and clear your mind. Remember that the MeChip is altering your perception. Keep that notion of deception at the front of your thoughts and continue observing the flowers. What do you see now?"

"The same flowers and vase," Alex replied, still puzzled. Was this a test of some sort, he wondered to himself? Unbidden came the thought he had harbored earlier, the suspicion Locke might be a little crazy.

"Keep looking at them, please. And remember, the MeChip is trying to alter your perception."

Feeling a little silly, Alex kept gazing at the flowers, which for their part remained still and silent in the vase, apparently unmoved by his hard stares.

"Keep going. And keep thinking about the MeChip," Locke insisted.

Alex maintained his focus on the flowers while simultaneously trying to think about the deceitful MeChip. Still nothing happened.

He was about to give up when the object in front of him began to shimmer and distort. As he gazed in amazement, it morphed and reformed into something else, something he hadn't expected.

"What do you see now?" Locke asked excitedly, noticing Alex's changed expression.

"The flowers are all dead, wilted and decayed."

"And the vase?"

"Different. Old and cracked."

"How about the smell?"

"It smells bad now, like food that's gone off."

"Good. Now look around the room. What do you see?"

"Still the new appliances. No, wait, they're changing too. It's the old ones again. The General Electric oven. The old white fridge."

"Good, good. Now return again to the flowers. Do you still see them as they really are; old and dead?"

"Yes."

"Alright. Keep looking at them. Let's see how long you can hold this image."

Alex continued staring at the flowers, noticing from the corner of his vision that Locke was now looking at his watch.

For some time, the flowers remained the same, decayed and lifeless. Gradually, though, Alex felt a surge of pressure around his head and neck, and the flowers flickered suddenly back to life. Alex fought the MeChip's influence, bringing the flowers back again to their true, but lifeless, form. Still the pressure mounted. For some time, the images blinked back and forth between the dead and living blooms as Alex struggled to maintain his concentration. Finally, though, he lost the battle and looked away. His breath was coming in ragged gasps and he realized he was sweating.

"I lost it," he admitted. "How'd I do?"

"Three minutes, ten seconds. Quite remarkable," Locke said, smiling. "I was impressed when your mind broke the MeChip's control at its first attempt. But to hold it for three whole minutes is really something. The MeChip is designed to make you see the world as better than it is. Those images are appealing and seductive, hard to break down. But you did it."

Alex smiled back, feeling a glow of pride.

"So I did well, then?" he asked, feeling oddly keen for more praise from this enigmatic old man.

"Oh yes, Alex. With training, you'll be able to spot the real image from the fake and resist subliminal control or even direct commands from the Fixers, even with your MeChip fully switched on. You have a strong mind, Alex."

"Can I try something else?" Alex asked, suddenly struck by an idea.

"Be my guest," Locke said, evidently intrigued.

Alex concentrated on the flowers once more and, after a few seconds, managed to transform them from their beautiful, fake MeChip reality into their true form, drooping and decayed. But he didn't stop there. As he continued to stare at them, he willed his MeChip to alter their form, not into pretty flowers but into a different shape, something else he wanted to see. Shimmering in front of him, the flowers morphed first into a cactus, then gradually, bending to Alex's force of will, into an owl. It sat there, its wide eyes staring at him, then fluttered its wings. At his mental order, the owl rose up into the air, flew around the room, and landed in its original spot. Exhausted, Alex finally let the creature revert back into flowers.

When Alex explained what he'd done, Locke could barely believe it.

"You mean you manipulated the MeChip image with just your mind, bent the MeChip to *your* will rather than the reverse. Are you telling me the truth?" he asked excitedly.

"Yes, I promise!" Alex said.

"Well, that is worth pondering. If we could somehow give you access to other people's MeChips and you could control them ..." Locke said to himself, obviously thinking hard. Finally, he shook his head.

"Well, Alex, you have shown your mind is strong. What you have done may offer us some possibilities. It requires more thought. In the meantime, I wish to tell you about the plan I have already devised, a plan that will help us fight back on a much larger scale."

Locke was about to explain when he was interrupted.

Bang! Bang! Bang!

"Open up!" came a loud, commanding voice from outside as soon as the knocking ceased.

Locke and Alex sat frozen, staring at each other in shock.

Bang! Bang!

"Open up, now! This is the Regulators. Official business!" came the same voice, louder now, as Alex looked at Locke in dismay.

It was obvious what had happened, Alex realized. Their attempts to evade capture had failed. They had been found!

Chapter Twenty-Three
The Regulators

"What should I do?" Alex demanded of Locke as he felt himself start to panic. "Hide?"

"No," Locke replied firmly, reaching for his remote. "Wait here. But be ready for anything."

"But it's the Regs—the cops! They've obviously found us ... found me!" Alex protested, feeling as if he should already be heading for the hills.

"I said wait here, Alex," Locke said sternly, rising to his feet and walking towards the front hall.

A moment later, Alex heard the door open and Locke's voice—friendly and calm—drifting back down the corridor.

"Good morning, officers. How can I help you today?"

"Good morning, sir. Look at this photo, please. Have you seen these two people: an old man and a teenage boy?"

"Hard to say, officer," came Locke's reply. "My eyesight isn't what it was, I am afraid."

"Well look again, old timer," the Reg replied, less politely this time. "We need to find these two. They may not look it, but they're dangerous crims."

There was a pause of several seconds and Alex imagined Locke must be making a show of perusing the picture.

"I don't think I can help you, officer," Locke said finally.

"Alright, well if you ..."

The Reg stopped speaking and again there was silence for several seconds. Still sitting at the kitchen table, Alex strained desperately to hear what was going on.

"... say, you look a lot like the old guy in the photo yourself," the Reg said finally, his voice no longer remotely polite but full of suspicion.

"Really? I would have thought I was a bit better looking, personally," Locke replied. "More distinguished, perhaps?"

"No, he looks just like you. You'd better let us in the house. We'll need to look around."

"I don't think so, young man," Locke answered.

"Step aside, old timer," the Reg said, suddenly sounding very serious.

A moment later, two Regs entered the kitchen. They were dressed in the standard Regulator uniforms—a peaked cap with a silver eagle button on the front, long black leather jacket with light grey epaulettes on each shoulder, dark pants and tall leather boots, as well as a baton, a pair of handcuffs, and the standard-issue Colt laser-pistol Mark 2, with its stun and kill settings, nestled in a black holster with silver trim. The male Reg was tall with a reddish-brown moustache clipped short at the sides; his female companion had curly black hair pulled back in a pony tail. The two of them saw Alex as they entered, their eyes flicking down to the photograph then back to the boy in the kitchen. They exchanged a glance and nodded to each other, a look of grim satisfaction on their faces.

"I think we got our crims," announced the woman, reaching for her Colt.

"I can't let you do that," Locke said as he appeared behind them. He was holding the remote now and, before either could react, pressed two buttons in quick succession.

The effect on the two Regulators was instantaneous.

"Um, what were you saying?" the first Reg asked slowly, his eyes unfocused.

"I'm not sure," said the second, looking as glassy-eyed as her partner and letting her gun slide back into its holster.

"I think you were saying we look nothing like the crims you're seeking. Nothing at all," Locke suggested gently.

"Oh, yeah. Nothing like," the first Reg said.

"You were saying everything is in order and perfectly normal here. So normal you will forget all about it as soon as you leave the house."

"Yeah ... perfectly normal here," the first Reg repeated dully.

"Forget all about it," the second said sluggishly.

"Let me show you out. Thank you for coming, officers. Good luck with your search," Locke said as he led them back out of the kitchen. A moment later there was a loud click as the front door closed behind them. Locke reentered the kitchen, the ghost of a smile on his face.

"That was amazing!" Alex said.

"Thank you," Locke said, nodding slightly.

"You saved us again, just like last night with the Fixers," Alex said.

"Actually, this was a little different. Last night I immobilized them—made them freeze. What I did to the Regulators just now involved planting new thoughts in their heads, which required rather more complex programming on my little gadget here."

"But I'm confused," Alex said as a new thought struck him. "Shouldn't the Regs and the Fixers be immune to your gizmo? Don't they work for the elites?"

"Yes, but they're not considered important enough to be in on the MeChip's terrible secret. Except for their most senior leaders, they all wear MeChips and are controlled by them. In fact, they're just as much their victims as anyone else, which means my little device here can work on them—at least in a small way."

"What do you mean, 'a small way'?" Alex asked.

"I mean it can affect two or three people at a time, if I'm lucky. But it does not have the power to control a larger group."

"Then how can we help more people, help everyone get free of the MeChip? Isn't that what you want?"

"Yes, that is my plan. I think I've figured out how to help the wider populace rise up against their controllers in larger numbers," Locke replied.

"Will it use the same technology as your remote? Can you make it more powerful or something?"

"No. At least, I haven't found a way to achieve that so far. Neither does my plan exploit that weakness—the ability to break the MeChip's control—that you showed an aptitude for before the Regulators arrived. Sadly, that skill would be even harder to train people in large enough numbers to make any difference at all. The Fixers would discover us before we could teach enough people to resist. No, it is the MeChip's other vulnerability, its other flaw, that is at the heart of my plan. And you, Alex, are at the center of it all," Locke said, looking at him earnestly.

Chapter Twenty-Four
Slade Arnold

"What do you mean?" Alex asked. "How can I be important in this? I'm just a teenager, just ... *me*."

"To explain things properly, I have to take you back in time to when the MeChip was first created," Locke began, stroking his beard and looking away, seemingly lost in a memory.

"Imagine me as a much younger man—hard as that might be now I am so old," he began, his eyes twinkling mischievously.

"Alright," Alex said, smiling back.

"It is more than twenty years ago. I am Dr. John Locke, no longer young but still in my prime, not this elderly shopkeeper you see today but the celebrated Chief Technology Officer for Happy Corps, the world's biggest technology company. I have recently invented the MeChip and it is already a sensation, my greatest creation and the fastest selling consumer product in history. It is making everything that came before it—smart phones and glasses, tablets, flatscreens, Bluetooth technology, literally everything—obsolete overnight. It does all they can and more. Every other piece of consumer technology is irrelevant and out of date. Nothing can compete with my newest and finest invention. Of course, everyone wants one! Happily for the world's nine billion eager consumers, Happy Corps is selling it at a reasonable price, knowing it can capture the market completely if it moves fast enough."

"Okay," Alex nodded, trying to imagine how it must have been.

"I have just been named Time magazine's person of the year, the nightly talk shows are lining up to interview me and universities are clamoring to give me honorary degrees. It was, I must admit, a most enjoyable time," he said, his green eyes sparkling with pleasure at the memories he was sharing.

"Then something even more momentous occurs. During one of my weekly meetings with Bill Phillips, Happy Corps' CEO, we are joined by someone much more important than either of us. Let me show you who paid me a visit," Locke said, standing up and walking over to a drawer as he spoke. Alex watched as his companion pulled out what looked to Alex like an old-fashioned, oversized book. He brought it to the table and set it down in front of Alex, blew the dust off the cover and starting flipping over the sheets. With interest, Alex realized it wasn't a book at all but an old-fashioned photo album.

Alex caught brief glimpses of pictures with Locke as a boy, then as a younger man, with other figures he assumed were friends and family. Finally, Locke stopped on a page showing three men together. One was Locke himself, perhaps in his early forties, looking fit and fashionable in a suit and tie. Standing next to him were two older gentlemen. Alex vaguely recognized the former CEO of Happy Corps, now retired, while the other man, smiling confidently at the camera, was ...

"President Donaldson!" Alex exclaimed in surprise.

"Correct," Locke said. "This was taken early in his first term during his secret visit to me. At that moment I am, of course, impressed and honored by his interest in my work."

"Who wouldn't be?" Alex agreed, remembering what he'd learned in class about the first President Donaldson, how impressive he had been and how much he'd done to restore America to its former power and glory. If all that was true, of course.

"Imagine this; President Donaldson Senior and Happy Corps' CEO come to me with a proposal and a challenge. Can I make a control mechanism for the MeChip, they ask, something to give us computer techies—and the government—the power to control how people see the world through the MeChip?"

"Did you ask them why?" Alex asked, starting to see where this was going.

"Of course. President Donaldson explains that it is just a precaution, something to make sure the MeChip cannot be hacked by a foreign power or powerful criminal gang. It is merely something to give Happy Corps and its friends in government the power to override anything someone with evil intentions might try to do to the MeChip. Which makes sense ... in a way."

"So you did it, then?"

"Of course. It takes a lot of work—two years' intense effort, in fact. It seems worth it at the time, however, not only to help the President but also for the sheer joy of testing my talents to their limits. It even brings me this," he said, walking back over to the drawer where he'd kept the photo album and returning to the table with another object, which he again set on the table in front of Alex: a blue sash and an intricately carved medallion displaying five golden eagles around thirteen painted gold stars.

"Is this a Presidential Medal of Honor?" Alex asked, eyes wide.

"Yes, the highest civilian award in America," Locke said, his tone oddly flat.

"But this is amazing!" Alex said. "You must have been so proud."

"I was. Not now, though. But let me finish my story," Locke said, holding up a hand to stop Alex, who had opened his mouth to ask another question about this prestigious object.

"The medal is ridiculous really, since these things are always a team effort. My greatest ally at Happy Corps by that time is a young man I'd recently hired as my number two, a genius perhaps even more gifted than I am myself. Coincidentally, we had come from the same town and even attended the same university, although he was more than ten years younger than me. His name is Slade Arnold."

"Slade Arnold? Why does that sound familiar?" Alex asked.

"Because he is an important and famous man. He is also the man you met last night."

"Last night?" Alex asked, confused.

"Yes. He was the one in charge of the Fixers who came to snatch you away. The one who knew my name."

"Oh ... right," Alex said, not sure what to make of this information. "So he's still working for them after all this time, then?"

"Of course. He's one of the most powerful men in the country. General Arnold, head of the Fixers—or the Reparative Patriotic Security Service, to use their official name. The Fixers are his enforcers, a shadowy group who maintain this entire web of lies and deception. They are the ones who uphold the illusion that America is healthy and happy, the ones who reprocess people, steal children from their natural parents, dispose of the dead and remove those who are dying from the pollution and terrible work conditions."

"And Slade Arnold is in charge of them?"

"Yes. But he is much more than that. Arnold is respected and even feared by others in the elite. He is on the board of Happy Corps and a member of the all-powerful President's Council. In fact, he—"

Bang! Bang! Bang!

Locke stopped in mid-sentence as the door sounded to another round of loud raps. Who was it this time, Alex wondered, as his feeling of panic started to return.

Chapter Twenty-Five
Pizza and Pollution

"How odd," Locke muttered to himself, frowning. "We really are popular today, aren't we?" he said as he rose from his chair, walked briskly to the window and pulled back the curtain slightly, peering out.

"Stay here," he said curtly.

"But—"

"It will be fine," he answered as he left the kitchen. A moment later, Alex heard the door open again.

"Pizza delivery," came a gruff, harsh voice.

"We didn't order any pizza."

"I have it here, 19 Lexington Avenue."

"Let me see that. I think it says 79, not 19. Look."

"Oh ... sorry. My mistake."

The door closed and a moment later Locke reentered the room.

"Wrong house?" Alex said, looking at him.

"Apparently ..." he said, his forehead corrugated into a series of deep, horizontal lines.

"Something wrong?"

"I'm not sure. I don't think so. At least, I don't see how it could be ..." Locke said abstractedly.

"You were telling me Slade Arnold was your protégé?" Alex asked at last, eager to hear more of the story.

"Oh yes, that's right. My protégé and my friend," he replied, still sounding distracted.

"And what happened then?"

"Oh ... well, I began to develop misgivings about the control mechanism," Locke said, shaking his head and looking at Alex once more. "As we worked on it, President Donaldson and Happy Corps' CEO kept a close eye on us, closer than if it was just some simple security feature. And they started asking Slade Arnold and I to add additional features, features any fool could see might be abused by someone reckless or ruthless enough."

"Like what?"

"Well for one, the ability to make people using the MeChip see a rose-tinted world—the world you have lived in your whole life—that makes everything seem better than it is."

"Anything else?"

"Yes, the power not only to protect the MeChip from hackers, but to implant ideas or thoughts directly into the user's brain without their knowledge or consent. That didn't feel right to me at all."

"What did you do about it?"

"I started asking questions. Too many apparently, because they eventually reassigned me to another project and put Slade in sole charge of developing the control mechanism. Within a year, they'd promoted Slade to joint Chief Technology Officer alongside me, making him my equal at the company. It was obvious even to me that I was being slowly sidelined."

"And what happened then? With the MeChip, I mean."

"I lost track of what Slade had achieved after that—or should I say, I was deliberately kept at arms' length. But I was soon to find out."

"What do you mean?"

"It happened on election night fifteen years ago. As the evening wore on, it was clear Donaldson was about to lose the election. The exit polls were coming in and he was way behind. People obviously didn't like his handling of the pandemics and the economy was in tatters. The rich were getting richer and most everyone else was suffering. So, the people voted him out after one term."

"But he was president for three terms before his daughter took over, everyone knows that," Alex said, gently correcting the old man.

"Everyone *thinks* they know that. In truth, that election was the night Happy Corps and the President flipped the switch and activated the control mechanism."

"So they changed the result?"

"Yes," Locke nodded solemnly.

"They cheated!" Alex protested.

"Yes."

"But that's not ... not democratic. Someone else should have won; the other candidate ... what was her name again?" Alex asked, trying to remember this obscure figure from history.

"Francesca Delano," Locke replied.

"Yes. But wasn't she a crazy radical: a communist or something?" Alex asked.

"Is that what they teach you in school?" Locke laughed bitterly. "No, she was quite middle-of-the-road, really. Her policies were less revolutionary than the Republican Teddy Roosevelt or the Democrat FDR, both of whom are remembered as American patriots. She simply wanted those in power to share more of their wealth. But the elites didn't want that. They wanted even more money and power for themselves."

"So what did you do? After they stole the election, I mean?"

"Nothing," Locke said, avoiding Alex's gaze. "The security forces came for me that night. Arnold was running them by then and suspected I might try something. I escaped and went on the run but was apprehended a week later. In the end, Slade Arnold was quite merciful, really. I was allowed to live but forced to formally "retire" from public life. I moved here, to your town; it seemed quiet and pleasant enough, and I had had family here at one point so knew it fairly well. It suited Arnold, too, to have me some distance from the center of power."

"So Arnold betrayed you?"

"Yes. But more importantly, he betrayed America. He was seduced by wealth and power. Like many of the elite, he thought he was superior to his fellow Americans, better than the other 99 percent. He no longer believes in democracy and equality, the things that made us great in the first place."

"And you couldn't make him change his mind, make him realize that what he was doing was wrong?"

"Sadly, no. When I tried, he told me I had turned soft. He viewed me as weak and sentimental and foolish for my misgivings about the MeChip. He sees Americans as sheep to be ruled and controlled, not as equals. He had no hesitation in pushing me aside and terminating our friendship. In fact, before last night I had not spoken to him in more than fourteen years."

They were silent for a while as Alex thought about what he'd just heard. It seemed so repulsive, so *un*American. Only, he realized dismally, this *was* America now.

"Dr. Locke, how bad are things, really?" Alex asked eventually. "I mean, I saw the smoky air and the trash and stuff when you turned my MeChip off outside your shop and when we drove here. Is it like that everywhere?"

"Everywhere except where the rich live, yes. Where people are under the MeChips' control, they are forced to work too hard in places where the pollution gets worse by the day and where schools and hospitals are left to decay. Look at what happened to your neighbor Mr. Adams. His death was a direct result of the elites and their misrule."

"Abby's dad? How?"

"Is it not obvious, Alex? That man was living in a city where the air is polluted, where the water systems aren't properly maintained and where viruses and other diseases are spreading. He was probably working long hours in an unsafe and dangerous job. It is no wonder people are dying younger. The Fixers who replaced him are only getting busier as time passes."

"But why don't the elites do something about it? I mean, surely they care a little?"

"Not enough to act, Alex. It is easier—and much more profitable—to leave things as they are and allow people to suffer and die, while the rich live in their beautiful, clean and safe gated communities—their shining sanctuaries of wealth and privilege above the squalor and decay the rest of us are forced to endure."

"That's disgusting," Alex said, remembering Abby's father coughing up blood. To know the elites did nothing to stop the pollution and disease that had almost certainly killed him made Alex feel a surge of anger.

"Dr. Locke, why have you waited all these years to do something about it?" he asked finally.

"Because Arnold was right. I was soft, weak ... and a coward. I let the country suffer because I was afraid of what would happen to me if I opposed it. I was also deeply depressed—overwhelmed, in fact—not only at what had happened to the country I love but at my own part in developing this dangerous technology."

"So what changed your mind? Made you want to fight back at last?"

"I cannot tell you, Alex. At least, not yet. For now, all that matters is I have decided it is time to stand up to them, time to exploit the MeChip's fatal flaw."

"What is its flaw?" Alex asked eagerly.

"The MeChip's shortcoming is also Slade Arnold's, which is why I wanted you to know more about him. It is a defect he would dispute, something he would not even consider a weakness."

"And that is ... ?"

"Feelings."

"I'm sorry?" Alex said, thinking he'd misheard.

"Slade Arnold thinks feelings and emotions make you vulnerable. He thinks of love as a failing. Cold, hard reason and power are his gods. He never understood that our emotions, our sentiments are what make us human."

"But why does this matter for the MeChip?" Alex asked, still confused.

"Because Arnold discounts our emotions it means he has also undervalued their importance in the MeChip design."

"That's not true," Alex argued. "After all, the MeChip is so strong people can be replaced and no one seems to notice, not even loving family members," he said, thinking of Abby's father and of his own parents, now probably harboring a surrogate son in their home.

"That is true. Slade Arnold did a good job fixing that particular problem. But there are parts of our minds—of our hearts and souls—the MeChip still cannot reach. This is partly because Arnold does not understand those parts of our nature. He does not realize that when we are touched by something creative and artistic, something sublime in its beauty, the MeChip loses its sway over our minds. In the face of such beauty, it can be neutralized, even short circuited."

"Do you mean like ... paintings or sculptures or something?" Alex asked, still unclear.

"Possibly that kind of art, yes. I admit I have not tried that particular path," Locke admitted. "But there is one creative outlet I have experimented with, one I know will work under the right conditions. It is something you yourself are passionate about," he said with the ghost of a smile.

"You don't mean—" Alex said, already guessing the answer.

"Yes, Alex. The MeChip's greatest weakness is music."

Chapter Twenty-Six
The Guitar

"Music? But we play music all the time and nothing changes," Alex said after pondering this for a moment.

"That is perfectly true. Not just any music will work against the MeChip."

"Then what?" Alex asked.

"The music must be inspirational, beautiful, powerful, something that will stir our emotions so strongly the MeChip cannot cope. Your modern, superficial stuff won't work."

"Not even Thrashtech or Rock Shop?" Alex asked, feeling a little disappointed.

"I am afraid not, Alex. And the music must be played on real instruments, too."

"We *have* real instruments," Alex insisted.

"Sadly, that is not the case. The new laser guitars and keyboards were deliberately designed by Happy Corps so they cannot affect the MeChip. Early on, you see, they noticed there were problems when truly inspiring music was played."

"So they know its weakness, then?"

"Arnold knows the MeChip is vulnerable to quality music, yes. But he never truly understood why, never tried to figure out how such sounds could counteract the MeChip. Instead, he just designed new instruments and speakers that could *not* stop the MeChip functioning. He suppressed the best of the old music and destroyed all the real instruments he could find, replacing them with new, plastic junk. These produce noises that are just a pale imitation of how true music sounds.

But real music played on genuine instruments by great musicians can still break the MeChip's control. Music that speaks to our hearts and souls reaches a part of us the MeChip cannot. Music can liberate us, set us free," Locke said, his green eyes shining.

Alex said nothing. Did this really make sense, he wondered?

"And this, Alex, is where you come in," Locke continued after a pause. "You must perform at the Best Band contest tonight. Most of the town will be there and I have a plan for you to reach a bigger audience ... much bigger, in fact. If you play tonight, you can break through the MeChips' control and free a great many people," he concluded, his voice now elevated and eager.

"But how? I don't mean to burst your bubble, but I'm not a great musician. I'm such a dexter I couldn't even play a single note last time I entered the contest. Iggy's much better than me."

"No. While he has talent, Iggy Elgar is not the one. You are. Look at me, Alex! You have greatness in you. Your mother saw it and I do, too. It is there, waiting to be unlocked. You only have to believe," Locke said, holding Alex's eyes with his own.

"But I don't know any old music, only the Synthipop and Thrashtech and Rock Shop stuff you say's no good."

"That is true. But there is still time. Look, it is not even 11:30 a.m. yet," he said, showing Alex his watch. "Here is some sheet music for you. Study it. Learn it. It has inspired millions in its time, although it has been hidden away and forgotten by the traitorous elite that rule our country today."

Alex took the old-fashioned pages and started to peruse them. As he read the music and the lyrics that accompanied it, his mouth slowly spread into a smile.

"Oh. This looks ... good. Great, actually. But how can I play it? I only have my synthi-guitar and you said it won't work. Besides, it's at my house. I don't see how we could get it now."

"Wait here," Locke said, rising from his chair and leaving the room. A moment later he returned with a black guitar case, which he set on the table. "Go on, open it," he said, smiling.

Alex unlatched it and pulled back the top. Inside was a stunning, six-string electric guitar. The words *Fender Stratocaster* were engraved in small letters on the headstock. Painted red and white with blue trim, it shimmered in the sunlight that slanted between the curtains. It was like nothing Alex had ever seen before and he realized with a jolt that Locke was right: this was a true instrument; his own synthi-guitar still lying in his bedroom at home was just a toy, a childish imitation of the genuine article. Alex lifted it out of the case, noticing the greater weight and beautiful craftsmanship of this real instrument. He stroked the strings reverentially.

"Alex, this instrument is for you," Locke said solemnly. "It is rare, one of the last of its kind in this entire state, although you have seen another."

"It's smeckin' amazing. Thank you."

"Now you must practice, Alex. A real guitar will take some adjustment compared with your cheap, modern ones. It needs tuning manually, for instance. And you'll need a real amp. I have a small one in the garage, but there is a much bigger and better one at your school, behind the stage in the main auditorium, ignored and unused behind the newer synthetic amps. Now, let's get to work," Locke said, suddenly businesslike. "We have much to do before this evening arrives."

Chapter Twenty-Seven
Removing the MeChip

Alex was in heaven. For two hours, he got to play this guitar. While much heavier and more solid than anything he'd used before, he soon got used to its weight and the thickness of the strings. Then the fun began.

First, he learned the song Locke had given him, reciting it to the old man perfectly after about 30 minutes or so. After that, Locke had given him two more books of sheet music. The first was of musicians he'd never heard of, with names like Lennon, McCartney, Mercury, May, and Sumner. The second was of even more ancient composers with unpronounceable names like Debussy, Chopin, Beethoven, and Mozart. As he read the music and tried out a few compositions from Lennon and McCartney, he was stunned at their sheer brilliance, at the originality and creativity.

Eventually, Locke dragged him away for a late lunch of sandwiches and root beer, which the old man had rustled up for them.

"How are you coming along?" Locke asked.

"I love it! I can't believe people could write music like this."

"Good. While you have been practicing, I have started to put more links in the chain of my plan," Locke said, smiling. His choice of words triggered a memory in Alex.

"Speaking of chains, last night Slade Arnold threatened to do something to you. Was it chainseek?"

"Chain*stitch*, Alex. You are quite right to ask about it. Chainstitching is a technique the Fixers use to punish those who are particularly troublesome."

"What do they do?"

"They sew the MeChip deeper under your skin, making it impossible to remove. Then they torture you with sights and sounds that drive you mad."

"It sounds terrible," Alex said, wishing he hadn't asked.

"It is. I have seen it happen. As you know, the MeChip usually implants fake images that are happy, since the Fixers find it easier to control people this way. But the MeChip can also implant negative images. Rather than making things look better than they really are, imagine if they were worse, if the flecks of old paint on the walls around you became giant spiders, or your dreams were twisted into your deepest fears and nightmares. Even in sleep there is no escape from the MeChip. Chainstitching gives the Fixers the ultimate mind control. It has turned this remarkable technology into a force for evil," Locke concluded, shaking his head sadly.

"Should I take out my MeChip?" Alex asked, horrified by the idea of chainstitching.

"It is probably a good precaution," Locke agreed, "not so much because I'm worried about you being chainstitched, Alex, but in case Happy Corps' top coders figure out what I've done to your MeChip and come up with a way to override it. We don't want your MeChip being hacked, do we?"

"Definitely not," Alex agreed.

"Here, let me help you remove it," the old man said, standing up.

"Okay," Alex replied, feeling strangely reluctant now the time had come. The teenager had to fight the urge to pull away as Locke walked behind him and he felt the old man's fingers at the back of his neck. Alex gripped the underside of his chair to stop himself from struggling as he heard the momentary sound of the tiny zip in his neck being pulled back and then felt the coin-sized chip being removed.

For a moment Alex wanted to scream out—not from pain, for it hadn't hurt at all physically—but from an overwhelming sense of loss.

It felt as if his soul had been sucked out of him leaving him an empty shell, a husk with a body but no spirit, no essence, no humanity left inside him.

Mercifully, the feeling only lasted a few seconds. As Alex drew a deep, slow breath, his sense of self returned along with something else, something more he couldn't quite identify. After that initial moment of panic and loss, he now felt lighter and happier. An unexpected question appeared in his head; in losing his MeChip, had Alex gained his freedom—his independence?

"Are you alright, Alex?" Locke asked, breaking into the young man's reverie.

"Yes, I'm fine now. But it felt weird when you took it out."

"It is not easy to let go of your MeChip. Even though I had disabled many of its features, the device would still have been implanting subliminal messages in your brain telling you to keep it in. This is why people almost never take them out. The MeChip doesn't *want* to be removed. It's one of Arnold's many acts of programming genius."

"That explains why I felt so reluctant for you to detach it," Alex admitted.

"But you *did* let me, which once again shows great presence of mind," Locke said, bestowing another smile on his companion. "That is twice you have bested the MeChip. Still, you should keep hold of it, just in case you need it again. Here," Locke said, handing the item to Alex before he could protest.

Alex looked at the tiny object in his hand. How could this small thing have caused so much pain and suffering to so many? It appeared so insignificant sitting there on his palm. For a moment, he felt a strange urge to throw it on the ground and grind it under his shoe. Then the moment passed. Carefully, he placed it in his jeans pocket.

"Without your MeChip we will need some other way to communicate," Locke was saying as he opened up yet another kitchen drawer, pulled out two identical objects and placed them on the table.

They were each almost the size of someone's hand, rectangular and made of some sort of black plastic.

"What are they?" Alex asked, looking at them with interest. "They're not more of those remote controls that turn off enemy MeChips, are they?" he asked eagerly.

"No. They're much older than that. They were once called 'smart phones' although compared to the MeChip they're really rather stupid. Still, they are good enough for communicating, especially now your MeChip is out. I have taken the liberty of programming in the number of my phone, so you will see my name appear on the device whenever I call you," Locke said as he showed Alex how to use this ancient technology. "I have also programmed in the numbers associated with the MeChips of a few of your friends like Sol and Tom, in case they call," he continued.

Alex looked through the list of contacts, stopping at one in particular.

"You have Abby Adams in here," Alex said quietly.

"What's that? Oh yes," Locke answered.

"Why do you have her number? She's not speaking to me anymore."

"Well, you never know if you might need it," Locke said, busying himself with the other phone as he spoke. Sensing something wasn't quite right here, Alex decided to persist.

"But why would I need to call Abby? Is something wrong? Is she in danger? You hinted at it last night, didn't you?"

Locke did not respond straight away but continued looking at the other phone, as if concentrating. Finally, though, he gave an answer that made Alex catch his breath.

"She may be in danger, yes. I try to monitor the Fixers' communications, when I can do so without detection. Lately, her name has been mentioned several times, although I cannot discover why.

What I do know is she is on their radar, which is why I thought it may be useful to add her number."

"Could it be because of me? Because they've been watching me and listened in on our conversations."

"I cannot say," Locke replied after a pause, looking once more at his phone.

Alex still had the impression Locke was holding something back. He was about to pursue the issue further when a sound came from outside that stopped them in their tracks: tires squealing as a vehicle braked suddenly. The noise came from directly outside the house. In an instant, Locke had rushed over to the window, pulled back one of the curtains, and looked out.

"Another misdirected pizza?" Alex asked, half smiling.

"Not this time, I'm afraid," Locke replied, his voice deadly serious.

"Do you mean—?"

"Yes, Alex. They are here. I am afraid we have been discovered."

Chapter Twenty-Eight
Flight to the Forest

"Alex, you must leave at once!" Locke began before his companion could react. "Here, take the guitar and sheet music. Go back to the bedroom and lift up the rug: you'll find a trap door. Open it and climb down. It leads to a tunnel that will take you into a field behind the garden. Use the flashlight on the phone to see your way. Once you're through the tunnel, run up the hill to Muir Forest. You should be safe there. And don't answer any calls! In fact, turn off the phone completely; if they've found us here, who knows what else they have figured out? And whatever you do, make sure you compete tonight in the Best Band contest. Everything depends on it!"

Locke said this all at a rapid speed, like a video clip that's played at twice the intended tempo. As he spoke, he stuffed the guitar and the music into the case and pushed it towards Alex.

Alex's reaction was the opposite of Locke's. Unlike the old man, who had immediately raced into high gear, Alex felt frozen.

"What are you waiting for?" Locke asked, frowning as Alex sat rooted to his seat.

"But I can't just leave you," Alex replied uncertainly.

"You must! I'll stop them, or slow them down at least. But you have to go. Now!" he said, half-pulling Alex out of his chair and shoving him in the direction of the bedrooms.

Smash! Crunch!

The sounds seemed to come from more than one direction and Alex realized their enemy must have split its forces. Clearly, the Fixers were trying to enter the house through both front and rear doors.

"Change of plan. Follow me," Locke said, leading Alex down the rear corridor. At the end of it stood the solid back door, which now had an ax head poking through it. The first splinters of wood scattered on the carpet as the ax disappeared momentarily from view, then smashed once more into the timber, flinging more fragments in their direction, although the door held firm for now.

"Into the bedroom and down the tunnel!" Locke urged, his eyes fixed on the damaged door. The old man fished the remote control from his pocket with one hand while shoving Alex into the room with the other. With one last look at his young companion, Locke pulled the bedroom door closed behind him.

Alone in the room, Alex tore back the rug, located the trap door, and pulled it open. It felt a little stiff, but a second tug loosened it and it swung back on hinges. Quickly, Alex descended down metal rungs into the darkness below, the guitar case held in one hand, until he finally reached the bottom.

"Get back! I'm armed!" Locke's voice drifted down from the house above, followed a moment later by a scream. Alex hoped desperately it wasn't the voice of his friend, but it was hard to tell from down here. Strapping the guitar case to his back, Alex pulled out the old phone and managed to turn on the flashlight. It revealed an earthen tunnel, a little damp in parts and propped up by metal framing. Alex had to stoop and take care not to hit his head, for the tunnel quickly shrank to less than five feet in height as he followed it. After descending slightly for a few steps, the passageway leveled out. He darted along it for another twenty paces or so before it turned slightly to the right then straightened out once more. He continued scrambling along as fast as he could for another forty of fifty steps until he finally came to a stop by another set of rungs built into the side of the ground and leading upwards to what Alex decided must be the exit.

He stopped for a moment, straining to hear any sounds from behind him. Was that another scream in the distance, or was it just his imagination? He couldn't be sure and this was not the time to wait and see. Grabbing the metal rungs, he started hauling himself up until he reached a circular metal grate above his head. It had an old metal bolt that kept it in place, locking it from the inside. The bolt seemed rusted and it took him several seconds to finally pull it free. He shoved at the grate and, grunting with the effort, felt it lift up and fall to one side.

Sunlight pierced his eyes, blinding him momentarily as he poked his head up and out of the shaft. Blinking furiously, his vision quickly adjusted and he took his bearings.

He was in a field. It looked unkempt, with weeds growing everywhere and old household junk—a rusty metal bed frame, a broken television, and numerous smaller items—scattered around the nearest fence. Behind the fence were the small gardens of a row of houses. The back door of the closest house looked like it had been broken down, and Alex realized this must be the dwelling from which he'd just fled. Turning to look in the opposite direction, Alex saw that at the far side of the field was a long, sloping hill covered in trees. This, Alex knew, was the edge of Muir Forest, a huge expanse of woods skirting one edge of the town and leading into a range of hills and, ultimately, mountains.

Without pausing to think, Alex pulled himself out of the hole and began sprinting towards the forest, just as Locke had ordered.

He was halfway across the field when he realized how incredibly exposed he was. Anyone coming out of the back door to Locke's house couldn't miss seeing him careering through the weeds and grass. Alex risked a backwards glance, almost tripping on the uneven ground, but there was no one at the back door and, as yet, no sign of detection or pursuit.

Finally, after what seemed like an hour but must in reality have been less than thirty seconds, Alex reached the safety of the trees. Even then he didn't pause, but plunged on and up the ever-steeper hill, not stopping until he had put perhaps half a mile between him and his possible pursuers. It was only when he'd reached the peak of the lowest in a series of small-but-rising hills that he paused, sat down on a convenient boulder, and tried to catch his breath.

His mind was racing as he thought back to what had happened. His first emotion was a surge of relief that he had evaded the Fixers' grasp once more. His second was guilt. Had he done the right thing in running away and leaving his companion behind? Sure, Locke had told him to do it; but was the old man just trying to be brave? Perhaps he, Alex, should have stayed and fought alongside him? Had he been a coward to run away? Well, it was too late to change his mind now, he realized ruefully.

He tried to remember Locke's hasty instructions. What had he said again? Compete in the Best Band competition, that was the main thing! He assumed Locke had meant for him to perform the song he'd given him the music to, and to use this guitar and the old amp he'd said was hidden backstage in the school auditorium. But what if the Fixers were waiting for him? Well, he'd have to deal with that when the time came.

What else had the old man said? Alex screwed his eyes closed and tried desperately to remember if Locke had given him any other instructions for what to do once he got away. With a flash, he recalled something else: the phone! Hadn't Locke said to turn it off so he couldn't be traced? Yes, Alex was sure he'd said something like that. Hurriedly, he pulled the antique gadget out of his pocket.

He was about to push the 'off' button when something quite unexpected happened.

Without any warning at all, the phone began to ring.

Chapter Twenty-Nine
The Call

B*rrr! Brrr! Brrr! — Brrr! Brrr! Brrr! — Brrr! Brrr! Brrr!*

The noise was loud and insistent, a series of three noisy chirps as the device trilled like a furious, high-pitched squirrel. There was a short pause followed by three more unwelcome rounds of the angry, nerve-jangling sound.

Alex looked at the phone.

Call from Sol Tubman, the display indicated, flashing on-and-off in time with the ringing.

What should he do? He was about to answer when he recalled something else Locke had said: don't answer the phone! But what if Sol was in trouble? What if there was an emergency?

As he stared at the display on the phone, he noticed the time: 2:37 p.m. That meant Sol should be in his last lesson of the day. Why would he be calling now if he was supposed to be in his History lesson? Something didn't add up. Coming to a decision, Alex pressed the button to decline the call.

He sat there in the suddenly silent forest, breathing in deeply to calm himself. He was some way up above the town now, and from his vantage point on the boulder he could see down into the wide valley he called home. A pall of smog hung over it and Alex could see the two towers of Happy Mining Company belching out black smoke. Even from this distance, the whole place had a run down, disheveled look to it, like a formerly fit, stylish person who has taken up smoking, started eating too much junk food, and generally let themselves go.

Brrr! Brrr! Brrr! — Brrr! Brrr! Brrr!

Alex jumped up as the phone rang again. He was about to end the call a second time when he noticed that this time it wasn't Sol.

It was Locke.

Was it really him, though, Alex wondered, hesitating? Perhaps the old man had defeated the Fixers all by himself? Or maybe he'd escaped? In which case, shouldn't he answer Locke's call so they could make their plans and arrange a rendezvous? But then, Locke had told him *not* to answer. And didn't they already *have* a plan?

Resisting the urge to take the call, Alex reluctantly hung up a second time.

He stood and peered down at Locke's house more than a half a mile away, straining to detect any movement or catch sight of someone emerging from the back door. Nothing.

Had he made the right decision? He was burning with curiosity to know what had happened. As he stood there, he now wished desperately he'd taken the call. Even if it wasn't Locke, even if it was some sort of trick, he couldn't stand not knowing what was going on.

He sat back down, his thoughts racing, his eyes still fixed intently on the distant house.

Should he call Locke back?

He picked up the phone, punched in Locke's name and brought up the number once more.

He was about to press the call button when he paused. Locke had definitely told him not to answer any calls. Surely *making* a call was even worse.

Wasn't it?

He was still sitting there staring at the phone when it surprised him by ringing for a third time.

Brrr! Brrr! Brrr! — Brrr! Brrr! Brrr!

Was it his imagination or was the noise even more insistent, even angrier, than before?

Then he saw who was calling and it drove every other thought from his brain.

It was not Locke this time.

It was not even his friend Sol Tubman.

It was, in fact, the last person he expected to hear from.

It was Abby.

Chapter Thirty
Chainstitched

This time he didn't even contemplate not answering. He knew what Locke had said. He knew he was not supposed to pick up. But this was *Abby*. He had to find out what was happening, had to make sure she was okay. Without pausing, almost as if it had a mind of its own, his finger instantly pressed the *answer* button.

It was her. Abby's face flickered into view and for a moment the two of them stared at each other.

"Abby, what's going on? Are you alright?" Alex said, fearing the worst as he noticed the dark smudges under her brown eyes. They had an uncharacteristically wary look, as if she was trying to hold back some strong emotion.

Before Abby could speak the image shifted and Slade Arnold's fierce face appeared for a moment before the camera—or whatever the device was—shifted to show the whole scene.

Abby was kneeling on the ground, hands tied behind her back. Next to her was Locke, also kneeling, also tied. Two Fixers stood close by, each holding a futuristic instrument that looked like a cross between a curved knife and Locke's old remote control with its tiny display and array of buttons. But Locke's device had no sharp, cutting edges, no obvious wickedness to it like these.

As Slade Arnold panned the device around to take in the rest of the room, Alex realized they were in the kitchen of Locke's safe house. Shocked as he was by what he'd seen already, his breath caught in his throat as he saw his mom and dad. They were not safe after all. Instead, they were standing impassively in the background, eyes at half-mast, chins dropped onto their chests just as they'd been when Arnold had switched them off the other night. Two more Fixers stood there flanking them.

"Are you watching, boy? Do you see this?" Slade Arnold asked as he swung the camera back towards Abby and Locke.

"Yes," Alex said, his voice barely a whisper.

"Then understand that you are responsible for all that is happening. Proceed!"

As Alex watched in horror, two Fixers inserted their hideous, sharp instruments into the back of Abby and Locke's necks, while two more held them firmly by their shoulders so they couldn't move, couldn't escape.

A terrible buzzing sound began, slow at first and then rising in volume and pitch as the device drilled into them. Unable to look away, Alex saw Locke grit his teeth and gasp in agony, while Abby screamed and slumped forward, unconscious but still held up by one of the grim Fixers.

Before Alex could react, Slade Arnold's face suddenly swung back into view.

"Did you see that, boy? They have been chainstitched because of you. Now their MeChips are under my complete control. Unless you surrender yourself to me I will torture them and make their lives an endless nightmare. And I will do the same to your mother and father, too, unless you give yourself up."

Alex couldn't move. He felt sick to his stomach and the scene started to sway.

"Did you hear me, boy?" Arnold said, raising his voice.

"Y ... yes," Alex just managed to reply, his voice so hoarse it came out barely above a whisper.

"Be at the train tracks next to Lincoln High Football Field at exactly seven o'clock tonight. If you are there on time then I will set them free. If not, you will condemn them to endless pain and I—"

"Don't do it, Alex!" Locke's voice cut-in suddenly from off-screen. "Hang up and turn off the phone. Stick to the plan! It's the only—aarghhh!"

The camera swung round once more to show Locke slumped forward, apparently unconscious. Then Arnold's face appeared again.

"Do as I say, boy! Be at the tracks by seven or they will all suffer. Obey my command!"

For a moment Alex remained paralyzed with fear. But something—whether it was Locke's words or seeing his friends tortured—spurred him to action. With an effort, he hung up and then turned off the phone completely. Then he picked up the guitar case, strapped it to his back, and began to run.

He knew he had to get away. Locke had said the phone might be trackable if it was turned on. Perhaps they had already traced him here?

Besides, he had to escape what he'd just seen. He started to sprint through the trees deeper into the forest, heedless of low hanging branches that cut at his face or tree roots that threatened to send him sprawling to the ground.

For a long time—he had no idea how long—he just ran. Ran to get away from it all: from the haunting images of Abby and Locke; from Slade Arnold's terrible threats; from this whole damned world and every smeckin' thing that had happened on this cursed and terrible day.

Chapter Thirty-One

The Forest

He finally pulled up near the top of a hill. His body felt utterly spent and his breath was coming in ragged gasps. His legs ached from running and his left cheek stung from a scratch courtesy of a low hanging branch as he'd careened wildly down a steep incline a few minutes earlier. He leaned forward, knees slightly bent and hands resting on his thighs as he tried to recover.

As his breathing started to slow, he looked around. Not far off was a group of large boulders that bore an uncanny resemblance to the last place he'd stopped. Had he been running around in circles? Was this the same hill as before? If it was, did that mean the Fixers could be waiting here to ambush him?

He took several steps slowly backwards into a clump of bushes, sank to his knees so he couldn't be seen, and tried to remain as quiet as possible. After seeing and hearing no sign of the Fixers for several minutes, he cautiously crept forward once more, looking from side-to-side as he advanced, then scaled the side of the largest and highest boulder.

Sighing with relief, he realized this was not the same place after all. For a start, he was some distance further into the forest now and was a fair bit higher up. Looking down and in front of him, he could clearly see the lower hill—the one he'd been on before—almost a mile away. Beyond it lay the town, now so remote the buildings looked like those miniature models enthusiasts often buy to go with their toy train sets or wargamer armies. From this distance, he could no longer see if any individuals were wandering around—could barely see the street where

Locke's house was—although the high towers of Bright Green Mining were still clearly visible as they continued to send dark smoke billowing high into the air.

Alex turned and looked behind him. A series of hills, each higher than the last, ascended into the distance, finally reaching mountainous, snow-capped peaks many miles away. Feeling he was safe, at least for now, he sat down, slipping the guitar case off of his shoulders and placing it carefully beside him on the huge rock.

In spite of his reckless charge through the trees, he had still not been able to outrun his own thoughts. His mind continued to race.

What should he do? He thought about Slade Arnold's ultimatum. Should he go to the train tracks at seven and give himself up, as he'd been ordered? Surely that was the right thing if it meant saving Abby, Locke, and his parents.

But would Slade Arnold keep his word? From what John Locke had said, General Arnold was a traitor to his country and could not be trusted. What if Arnold captured Alex but did not release the others? What if they all ended up chainstitched and tortured?

Meanwhile, what should Alex do about Locke's plan? His elderly friend had been quite clear that Alex should get to the Best Band contest at all costs. But would the plan even work now Locke was in the hands of the enemy? Who knew what other elements there were to Locke's idea? Whatever they were, they wouldn't happen now Locke himself was captured. Alex sat there for a long time, his thoughts rushing round and round without getting any closer to an answer.

Almost without thinking, he reached for the case and pulled out the guitar. Next, he set the sheet music in front of him and struck the first chord.

He rehearsed for a long time—perhaps an hour or more—before finally setting down the old instrument. He had no way of knowing the time now his MeChip was in his pocket rather than in his neck and with the antique, not-very-smart smart phone turned off.

He looked up into the sky. The sun was beginning to sink lower, although it looked like there was at least an hour or more to go until it fell below the horizon. Sunset around this time of year was sometime between 7 and 8 p.m., Alex knew. So he still had time, then.

Carefully, he placed the guitar and the sheet music back in the case, then sat there quite still, looking and listening. Unlike the sickly specimens in town, the trees here were tall and lush, their foliage turning red and orange and yellow as they took on their fall colors. Birdsong rang out intermittently and overhead Alex saw a majestic eagle as it soared high above him scanning for prey. A few yards away a family of deer walked out of a dense stand of trees, saw Alex, pondered his silent and unmoving figure for several seconds, then ambled on their way. The air here was clean and clear, with none of the smog and sickness that lay in plain sight in the valley below. For an instant, Alex imagined what life could be like if the people were free to choose their own path, a path in harmony with nature. Life without the MeChip might look terrible in the polluted towns, but perhaps it needn't be so bad after all if it could be like this.

As he took it all in, a sense of calm descended upon him, as if all the pieces of a particularly difficult puzzle had miraculously fallen into place.

He had made his decision now. For better or worse, he knew what he had to do.

He stood up again, strapped the guitar case to his back and turned towards town once again.

It was time to go.

Chapter Thirty-Two
Betrayal

The sun was low in the pinky-orange sky and the trees cast lengthening shadows on the sloping ground. Alex had reached the edge of the forest almost half-an-hour ago, then followed it around the periphery of town until he finally saw Lincoln High School's sports fields and buildings below him. Now they were just a few hundred yards away down steeply-sloping ground. At the front of the main school building, Alex could see the car park was full; he could just make out crowds of people threading their way inside. Lights blazed out of the old buildings to welcome the throng. Since the competition started at seven and folks were apparently still arriving, Alex guessed it might be around 6:45 or perhaps 6:50 p.m., which should give him plenty of time. He hoped.

Cautiously, he stepped from out of the trees and began picking his way carefully down the rock-strewn, weed-choked meadow, re-entering the pall of smog that lay over the valley as he headed in the direction of the school. Within two minutes he reached an old, barbed wire fence, fallen down in parts, which he stepped over, taking care to avoid the rusty metal. Then he continued in the direction of the school.

Any casual observer might have thought he was heading straight towards Lincoln High. That would mean, of course, that Alex intended to honor Locke's plan and perform in the contest rather than do as Slade Arnold had commanded, no matter what the cost to those in that cruel man's grip.

But this was not the case.

As Alex reached flat ground, he walked only as far as a train track. In one direction, the track led into the hillside and a dark tunnel just 30 or 40 yards away. In the other, it approached the school sports fields before turning away to the right and skirting the edge of the town. Alex stepped over the tracks so he was close to the sports fields. On the other side of the tracks was an old road that dead-ended nearby.

Hoping desperately that he'd done the right thing, Alex stood and waited.

For some time, nothing happened. Surely it must be seven by now, Alex thought? Had the Best Band contest started already? Alex could imagine the school's large auditorium packed to bursting with excited teenagers, parents, and teachers. If it was anything like last year's competition, Principal Ginsburg would be onstage wearing her favorite brown pantsuit and smiling over her reading glasses at the crowd as she welcomed them and introduced the contestants. Meanwhile, the bands would be warming up backstage, each now ready and waiting in their outrageous costumes. Alex was proud of the gear he had designed with Tom and Sol—a kind of cross between Sci-fi Glam, Rock Shop and the Revolutionary War. Some of the other seven bands would be just as ostentatious or garish. Alex hadn't seen Iggy's getup this year, but he guessed it would be something cool. Last year, they'd come as Thrashtech Mechwarriors. The winner, as always, would go on to the regional contest, and maybe even the nationals. Not that it mattered for Alex now, of course. Why was he even thinking about it? With an effort, he dragged his attention back to where he was.

There was still no one here. The train track was deserted and Alex began to wonder if he was late after all. Impulsively, he decided to turn the smart phone back on. After all, what did it matter now if Slade Arnold could track his whereabouts? The display glowed back to life and after a moment told him what he wanted to know: it was 6:59 p.m. As he continued staring at the screen, the numbers switched and the clock advanced by one minute: 7:00 p.m. Perfect timing.

As if on cue, two large black vehicles rounded a corner and came into view. They screeched to a halt at the end of the road. Doors swung open and Arnold and four Fixers stepped out with Alex's parents, John Locke and Abby in tow. The prisoners stood silent and dazed, as though in a trance. Alex thought he could see a thin line of dried blood starting in the corner of Locke's mouth and trailing down his chin.

Arnold stood looking at Alex from the far side of the tracks, his mouth curled in a mocking grin.

"Here you are, then," he said finally.

"Let them go, Arnold!" Alex shouted, trying to sound braver than he felt.

"Put your MeChip back in and you have my word they will be freed. You do still have your MeChip, don't you?" Arnold asked. Feeling strangely distant and detached—as if he was still watching and listening to events from the safety of the forest—Alex noticed for the first time that Arnold had the barest trace of an accent under his mostly-American twang. Was he originally English, perhaps? European? Well, no time to worry about that now.

"Did you hear me, boy? I said put your MeChip back in and they will be freed. I give you my word," Arnold said again.

Reluctantly, Alex complied, pulling the tiny MeChip from his pocket and checking that it was the right way up. It took him several seconds to reinsert it as he had to work by touch rather than sight to unzip the skin at the back of his neck and refit the device. Eventually, though, he managed to push it back into place, hearing just the faintest *click* as he did so.

The result was instantaneous. As he gazed about in wonder, the world around him shimmered and reverted to its rose-tinted view: the smog evaporated, to be replaced by a perfect Fall evening; the football fields behind him suddenly sported the latest astro-turf and high-tech gear, not the unkempt, neglected look they'd had just moments before; the High School buildings were not crumbling and dilapidated but gleaming proudly as the last of the Sun's rays stretched over the horizon, shimmering off glass and metal.

Alex had only a few seconds to take all this in, though, for General Arnold broke into his thoughts, his voice now amplified by the MeChip's power.

"Fool! Do you think I would keep my promise to a rebellious child? Now you will obey only me. Feel the force of my words. You will ... you *must* step across the tracks and surrender yourself to me!"

It was like nothing Alex had experienced before. The strength behind Arnold's command—its power unexpectedly magnified by the MeChip—was utterly overwhelming. Unable to resist, Alex took a step towards the track, then another and another, as Slade Arnold stood waiting for him, arms folded and his cruel grin growing, his victory now seemingly assured.

Chapter Thirty-Three
The Train

Alex tried to resist. Dimly, as if his brain was half-broken, he sought to summon the energy to fight Arnold's command. But all the mental might he'd shown at Locke's house had deserted him. General Arnold was too strong, the dominance of the MeChip too much. Alex took another step, then another, towards the tracks. Somewhere at the back of his consciousness, he was vaguely aware of something else: a distant rumbling, a deep vibration in the ground. But his mind was moving too slowly to comprehend what it might be. It didn't matter, anyway. All that mattered now was obeying Arnold's voice. That was everything now. It always would be, he realized hopelessly. He took another step closer.

"Don't do it, Alex. Escape! It's our only chance. Please, Alex, please!"

The voice carried forcefully across the tracks, snapping Alex back to wakefulness.

Slade Arnold spun around, staring in shock at the speaker.

It was Abby Adams.

"Impossible!" Arnold shrieked. "How are you breaking my command? Silence girl. Silence now!" he demanded imperiously.

As if the outburst had cost the last of her strength, Abby suddenly stood rigid, then her head fell slightly as all traces of resistance left her.

Still frowning but apparently satisfied, Arnold turned back to his Fixers.

"We need to end this. Grab the boy," he instructed them. Instantly, the Fixers started towards Alex.

But Abby's shouts had broken the spell. Feeling surprisingly clear-headed and revitalized, Alex strained his mind to fight off the MeChip's strength. With a supreme effort of will, he cut the General's control, at the same time reaching behind his neck and tearing out his MeChip. Now he was truly back in command of himself.

What should he do? Seeing there was no way to fight the gang of Fixers single-handed, Alex turned and began sprinting away from them towards the school football field. Meanwhile, the sound he'd dimly noticed earlier seemed suddenly louder—much louder—and he finally realized what it was: an approaching train.

"Stop him!" Arnold bellowed as Alex tore at top speed towards the school. Laser beams burst all around him as the Fixers began blasting. The sound of the train grew louder.

Something smashed into Alex's back and he felt himself lifted up into the air then, as if in slow motion, falling back to ground. The force of the blast took his breath away and twisted him round in mid-air. He landed face up, hearing a loud *crack* beneath him as he hit the earth. A laser must have shot him, he realized, and yet strangely he felt no pain. Is this what happened when you died? Did the agony go away?

With an effort, he lifted his head off the ground and saw two of the nearest Fixers only 40 paces away, both standing still and aiming their weapons at him, ready to fire again as he stared hopelessly up at the barrels of their raised guns. Meanwhile, the rumbling noise grew even louder.

Suddenly a huge object streaked past, bursting from the nearby tunnel at an incredible speed. It smashed into the two Fixers, hurling one like a ragdoll into the air and carrying the other away with it as if he'd never existed, while their two laser blasts fired well wide of their target—the last, failed act either of them would ever make.

The massive freight train—for that is what it was—reached its noisy crescendo as it thundered by and one railroad car after another continued to tear past in an apparently never-ending succession, sending wind and dust billowing in every direction.

Realizing the train was now a barrier between him and his remaining adversaries, Alex gingerly tried to stand up. He wasn't dead, he realized with surprise. He wasn't even dying. But the superb *Fender Stratocaster* guitar, which had been strapped to his back, was broken and charred by the laser blast. It had saved his life but paid the ultimate price. Meanwhile, the train continued to streak by, still separating Alex from his pursuers. But for how long?

What should he do? Thinking fast, he knew he couldn't fight Arnold and the two remaining Fixers. He also realized Locke had been dead right: Arnold could not be trusted. The man was the worst type of traitor.

That meant he, Alex, must run away and live to fight another day, as the saying went. Could he get back to the forest, perhaps?

Or was there something else he could be doing, something better than hiding and skulking? What about Locke's plan? Yet how could he carry out the plan if the guitar he was supposed to use was damaged beyond repair? Was there a replacement somewhere, another guitar he could use?

All of these were the thoughts of an instant. Then it hit him. In a moment of sudden inspiration, Alex remembered something important, something that changed his mind about everything. Nodding to himself, he turned his back on the train and his enemies and started sprinting once more towards the school, leaving the charred ruins of the guitar and its shattered, smoking case lying on the stony ground. But Alex had not given up everything, for in one hand was the sheet music, miraculously intact in spite of the laser blast, while in the other was the phone.

Chapter Thirty-Four

Mr. X

Alex didn't stop running until he'd crossed the sports fields and reached the back of the school. He was now at least 250 yards from his enemies. Casting a quick glance over his shoulder, he saw the last of the train's countless carriages speed out of the tunnel, meaning General Arnold and the others could resume the chase at any moment. Before they could spot him, he slipped through the gap between the changing rooms and the bike sheds, where he stopped for a moment, now out of sight of his foes.

He punched a name into the phone. It rang for several seconds before someone answered.

"Alex! Where the smeck are you? What's been going on? We haven't seen you all day and—"

"There's no time to explain! Listen, I'm on my way. Are you ready to perform? We didn't miss our turn, did we Sol?" Alex asked anxiously.

"No, we're here. We go on third, straight after *Iggy and the Overlords*. He's on next, following *Saratoga Redux*, so you've got maybe seven minutes, eight tops."

"Okay, I'll be there as soon as I can. And whatever you do, don't give up our spot. We need to perform. We have to!"

"Um, okay," Sol replied, speaking slowly. "Alex, what's going on, exactly?"

"I'll explain later, I promise. But listen, you need to get the old school amp—the really big, antique thing no one ever uses. It should be backstage somewhere. We have to use it. Okay?"

"Fine," Sol said, sounding exasperated. "But just so you know, you're doing it again."

"What?" Alex asked, surprised.

"Going all smeckin' Crazy-Clinton on us."

Alex didn't even know how to begin answering that, so he hung up, then switched off the phone for good measure.

He just hoped his friend came through for him with the amp. He could imagine Sol telling Tom about this call. He wouldn't blame either of them for thinking he'd gone Crazy-Clinton. What with his off-grid episodes, his faffing about over whether to enter the Best Band contest and his dextering behavior generally, it was probably the only thing that would make any sense to them. But there wasn't time to worry about that now. He still had something important to do.

Alex jogged towards the back of the main building, found an open window, and climbed through, letting himself into one of the corridors. Now he was inside, he could hear the sound of a band start-up on the far side of the building, the cheers of the crowd as the drums kicked off, then the applause as a guitar roared out.

It could only be Iggy. Only he had that strutting, cocksure Thrashtech sound so nailed down. As Alex started trotting towards his destination, he heard Iggy's voice ring out in the distance as he kicked-off their performance. Alex had overheard them practice only once in recent weeks, but this was a song he knew. The whole thing was pure Iggy: arrogant, overbearing, but so catchy and cool it was sure to win over almost any crowd. Iggy had written the lyrics himself, Alex knew, and taken the music from some obscure tune Alex barely recognized. Even from a few corridors away, he could hear Iggy's words ring out:

"God save our gracious Me,
Long live our noble Me,
God save the Me,

Send me victorious,
Happy and glorious,
Long to reign over you,
God save Iggy.
You know I'll take you there,
So good that it's not fair,
Just let it be,
Send me victorious,
Happy and glorious,
The prize should be belong to us,
Give it to Me.
So give me victory,
Rock God celebrity,
Let it be Me,
Don't hate my perfect hair,
Dexters know it ain't fair,
But I'm not going anywhere,
Give the prize to Me!"

Alex tried to ignore the song—which made him feel irritated and insecure in equal measure—as he entered a darkened classroom, closing the door quietly but firmly behind him. Instantly, the volume of Iggy's band diminished. Inside the room, instruments and other musical gear were lined up neatly along the walls, but Alex ignored these and made his way straight to the far end of the rehearsal room. There he looked up at the old mannequin, Mr. X, who was hanging there. The mannequin was still dressed in old jeans, boots, and a leather jacket, his featureless face illuminated in the moonlight slanting through a window. Gently, Alex slipped the old guitar off of Mr. X's shoulders and looked at it carefully.

He'd been right. This was what John Locke had said when he'd told Alex he'd seen another real guitar before. It was a second *Fender*

Stratocaster, this one x-shaped with a scarlet and white body tapering into a mahogany wood neck and headstock. It was obviously the genuine article, superior in craftsmanship and sound to everything except the one the Fixers had just blasted to bits. Alex blew the dust off its surface, feeling a touch of shame that he should ever have thought the modern, plastic trash that passed for instruments these days could be better than this.

"Thanks, Mr. X. I just need to borrow it for a while. I'll take good care of it, I promise," he said to the mannequin, looking up at it one last time.

He was just walking back towards the door, the *Fender* guitar cradled in his arms, when the sound of footsteps in the corridor made him stop in his tracks. A moment later came the flash of a laser blaster.

"What are you doing?" came a plaintive cry from the hallway, followed a moment later by another, more authoritative voice Alex knew at once.

"Stop firing, fool! Can't you see it's not him," came Arnold's command from somewhere down the passageway.

"Sorry, General!" muttered one of the Fixers, whose outline Alex could dimly make out from the other side of the glass in the door.

"Who are you?" Arnold asked the unseen victim as Alex continued to stand perfectly still in the room, hoping no one would peer in and see him.

"I'm William Wells, the janitor," replied a shaking voice. "Why are you shooting at me?"

"Have you seen a boy around here? Brown hair ... red and blue jacket?" Arnold asked, ignoring the man's question.

"No. Everyone's at the music competition," the man replied.

"Alright. Well, keep an eye out for him. And you will forget about the laser gun, do you understand? Forget it. Now!" Arnold said, his voice imperious as ever.

"Forget about it, forget about it," came the dazed and muted response in a voice Alex knew meant the MeChip was being used to control the man's mind and memories.

"Come on!" Arnold said, as several shapes rushed past the door and carried on down the corridor.

Cautiously, Alex approached the entrance and peered out to left and right. There was no one there. Luckily, Arnold and his goons had run in the opposite direction to the auditorium, but it was still with some trepidation that Alex began making his way once more along the passageways and towards the sound of the competition.

Now he was back in the corridor, he could hear Iggy's band finishing up a different song. Since each band was supposed to perform only one piece, Alex wondered if they'd done some sort of medley, merging one number into the next in order to bend the rules and show off more of their musical skills to the audience.

Whatever they'd done had clearly worked. As the band finished, the crowd went absolutely wild, cheering and shouting in obvious approbation.

"Thank you! Thank you! We are *Iggy and the Overlords* and we thank you for letting us rock your world!" echoed that arrogant voice Alex knew only too well.

More cheering, more applause came flooding up the corridor in waves as Alex made his way closer and closer, still keeping an eye out for the Fixers and their leader. How was his band going to compete with *that*, Alex wondered nervously? But winning the contest wasn't what this was all about now, he reminded himself sternly as he turned another corner and walked boldly backstage.

Chapter Thirty-Five

Iggy

"You're here!" Tom said as Alex walked into the backstage area. Gear was everywhere. Harriet, the bass player from *Saratoga Redux,* and a couple of other musicians were coming and going, but otherwise it was surprisingly empty except for Tom, who was grinning broadly at Alex's arrival. A moment later, though, Tom's face fell as he looked more closely at his friend.

"What the smeck happened to you? You look like you've been well-and-truly Tysoned!"

Alex looked down at himself, noticing for the first time the dust and dirt that covered his clothes and, no doubt, his face and hair.

"Guys, a little help here!" came Sol's voice as he emerged from around a corner dragging the huge, antique amp.

"Be right there!" Tom called over his shoulder. "Alex, you need to get yourself tidied up before coming onstage. Your uniform's right here," he added, nodding at a crate nearby with a large canvas bag on top.

"I don't care about the clothes now, I—"

"Just put on the jacket at least," Tom interrupted. "You look a mess! Here, give me your guitar and I'll set it up onstage for you." He took one last look at Alex, noticed the old guitar, stared at if for a second, shook his head in disbelief, then turned away to help Sol. Meanwhile, Alex could hear Principal Ginsburg at the mike and speaking with the crowd once more.

"And that was the remarkable *Iggy and the Overlords*. Thank you, Iggy! Next up is, let me see now ... oh yes, *Xander and the Plan A's*."

Alex heard a smattering of applause and a couple of people laughing as his friends entered the stage. Were they reacting to the oversized old amp, he wondered? Or were they remembering his humiliation from last year? No time to worry about it now. Instead, Alex walked swiftly over to the crate, pulled on the *uber* cool retro-Revolutionary War jacket that was the most important part of his stage gear, and started dusting off his clothes. He was about to try to tame his hair, which he realized was coated in filth from his fall near the rail tracks, when someone bumped into him. He spun around, half expecting to see Arnold or one of the Fixers, but it was a different sort of person entirely.

"Iggy!" he said, surprised.

"And the Overlords!" said one of Iggy's minions, leering at Alex over their leader's shoulder.

"Guys, I'll catch you up in a moment," Iggy said, glancing back at his friends. "I just want to ... um ... wish Alex here good luck."

"Don't be long, Iggy. We want to start celebrating our victory," said another minion as they slouched off in the direction of the boys' changing rooms.

"Isn't that a bit premature? You haven't won yet," Alex said.

"Well, it's pretty much preordained when you look at the competition," he said, staring down at Alex. "But listen, I want to give you some advice before you go onstage."

Iggy was about to continue when something made him pause.

"Oh, it's someone calling my MeChip. I need to take this. Give me a millisec," he instructed, then started listening to whomever was on the other end of the call.

"Um, Iggy, I'm supposed to be onstage so I'm just gonna go," Alex said, trying to step past his old adversary. But Iggy wouldn't let him by, reaching out and placing a hand firmly on his shoulder to hold him in place. Alex wasn't sure whether to try to push past, but after a few more seconds Iggy's MeChip call seemed to be wrapping up.

"Yes ... yes, I understand. You can count on me, sir," Iggy said quietly before turning back to Alex.

"Iggy, I really have to go. Listen!" Alex said, as the first sounds of an impatient crowd began to be audible backstage and a refrain of "*Why are we waiting? Why are we waiting?*" started to ripple through the audience.

"I don't think so, Alex."

"What?" Alex asked, confused.

"There's been a change of plan, see," Iggy said, an odd smile distorting his usually handsome face.

"What do you mean, Iggy? I thought you just wanted to give me some advice?" Alex asked. He had an odd feeling about this. A bad feeling.

"Yes, I was going to give you some advice about not being such a dexter. But that was before General Arnold called me just now on my MeChip," Iggy said, leaning down and picking up something that was placed against the nearest wall, hidden in shadow.

"General Arnold?" Alex said, not sure he'd heard right.

"Yup. He first contacted me a couple of weeks ago, told me you were some sort of traitor. Hardly a surprise," Iggy said, stepping forward as Alex saw what he had picked up from the ground—a heavy metal bar. "And now he says I have to stop you performing, even if that means hurting you bad."

"Iggy, listen to me! I don't know what he told you, but he's lying," Alex pleaded desperately. "It's Arnold who's the traitor. He's even kidnapped Abby. I can stop him, but only if I can get onstage. Please let me past, Iggy," Alex begged as the tall young man continued to bar his way.

For a moment Iggy looked confused, as if he was fighting some sort of internal mental battle. He frowned, stopped, shook his head several times, and appeared about to speak.

The moment passed. The MeChip's control mechanism had clearly won. Arnold was in charge now.

"Sorry, Alex. No can do," Iggy said firmly.

Without warning, Iggy swung the metal bar at Alex, who leaped backwards, tripped on some cables, and fell to the ground. Iggy was on him before Alex could even try to get back to his feet. He looked up at his old adversary as Iggy raised the bar above him to deliver a deadly blow. There was nothing Alex could do now, no way to escape. He'd come so close, he realized, as he closed his eyes and waited for the weapon to strike.

Chapter Thirty-Six
Revolution

There was a muffled, metallic sound as the weapon hit home, then a second muted thump. To his surprise, however, Alex felt nothing; no sensation of contact from the bar striking him, no crushing pain ... nothing at all.

Cautiously, he opened one eye, then the other.

Sol was there, a giant cymbal in one hand, while Iggy lay unconscious on the floor nearby. For a moment, neither of the two friends spoke.

"That was weird," Sol said finally, looking at Iggy's prone body without any obvious emotion. "Care to explain, Alex?"

"No time now," Alex said as Sol reached out and helped him to his feet. "But thank you."

"Any time. We better get onstage," Sol said as the sounds of the impatient crowd continued to grow louder.

"Did you set up the amp?" Alex asked as the two of them stepped forward.

"Yup, although it's an old piece of junk, you know," Sol replied.

"And the guitar?"

"That too, although that's even junkier. What the smeck are you doing with Mr. X's guitar anyway? Is this some sort of joke?" Sol asked.

"They're not junk, Sol. Far from it. And this is no joke, either. I'm about to start a revolution is all. Come on!"

"Why are we waiting? Why are we waiting?" The crowd was in full song now as Alex and Sol ran onstage.

"Thank smeck!" Tom said as his two friends emerged from the wings. "Is everything okay?" he asked as the audience caught sight of Alex and Sol, causing their loud refrain to peter out.

"Is everything okay?" Sol said, repeating Tom's question. "I guess that depends on whether Iggy trying to kill Alex with a metal bar is okay, or whether Alex wanting to perform using broken old gear that will land our reputations further in the gutter is okay? But if you don't mind that, then yeah, everything's just smeckin' peachy!" Sol said, finally starting to get worked up.

"Hey, look on the bright side. Whatever Alex has got planned can't be worse than what he did last year, right?" Tom said, grinning mischievously. "But anyway guys, we'd better start!"

Alex stood there, squinting under the bright stage lights as he tried to take his bearings. He picked up the guitar and grabbed a pick, noticing how clammy his hands felt. He tried to tune out the sounds of the crowd, to ignore the fact he was being watched by at least 1000 pairs of eyes as he checked the settings on the amp—which bore the word *Marshall* in large, loopy white letters over its black casing. He experimented with a chord. The *Fender* was tuned to perfection and the sound from the *Marshall* was clear and strong. Nodding to himself, Alex turned to his bandmates, still trying not to look at the crowd.

"So, are we doing our Rock Shop number?" Tom asked.

"Um ... no," Alex said. "Here's some sheet music. It's real simple; just basic drums, 86 beats per minute, and the bass line is straightforward, although really good. Take a look while I speak to the crowd. I'll lead us in. Sorry for the surprise, guys," he said as he stepped up to the mike leaving his two friends gawping at him open-mouthed.

As Alex approached the microphone the crowd fell silent. He gazed out into the sea of faces, hazy in the searingly bright stage lights, and stopped. As his eyes adjusted, he began to make out individuals in the crowd: Abby's friends Martha, Sally, and the red-headed Sybil, whom his friend Tom had said he liked. A little further back, his

English teacher, Ms. Monroe, her elderly face almost lost in the mass of students and parents, many of whom were much taller than her. Sol's parents, who were near the back of the hall. What would they all think about what he was doing? The moment seemed to slow as he noticed his rapid heartbeat, felt the adrenalin course through him as he realized fully for the first time where he was and what he was doing.

Unbidden, the memory of last year's events when he'd frozen onstage came flooding back as he stood quite still. His breath was coming in short, shallow gasps and his mouth felt dry. He licked his lips as he continued to gaze, petrified, into the overcrowded hall.

Anticipating a repetition of last year's humiliation, the crowd started to mutter among themselves. A few laughed. Alex licked his lips again and swallowed as he spotted General Arnold and two of his Fixers enter the hall at the back, with Locke, Abby and his parents still in tow. Time was running out.

Trying desperately to pull himself together, Alex drew a deep breath and began to speak.

"Good evening, everyone. I'm Alexander ... Alex to my friends, although my stage name is Xander. I'm here to start a ... well, a revolution." He looked out at the crowd, which had fallen silent at the exact same moment, as if it was one giant organism—its actions coordinated and synchronized—rather than 1000 separate individuals. Most of them looked confused at what he was saying. Before they could start talking among themselves again, though, he ploughed on.

"Um, where was I? Oh yes, a revolution. Well, *the* revolution, really. What I mean to say is that this moment might go down in history ... I suppose. I hope so, but, um ..."

He stopped once more, trailing into silence. Now the crowd was muttering again. This was not going well. They just didn't get it. He looked back at Sol and Tom, who seemed as baffled as everyone else. Shading his eyes from the bright stage lights with one hand, he scanned the crowd until he caught sight once more of Arnold, still stuck among the throng near the back of the room, struggling to move forward.

Then he saw her. She was behind Locke and his parents, whose eyes were cast down at the floor as they shambled along under the MeChip's control, pushed forward by the Fixers. But Abby was looking up. Looking at him.

Their eyes met and he sensed recognition in them. Had she managed to slip free of the MeChip's control again? She frowned, then with an effort gave him a small smile and nodded, her bright brown eyes shining with sudden awareness and confidence. In him.

Now he had all the support he needed. If Abby Adams believed in him, Alex knew he could do it. He leaned forward again into the mike.

"So where was I? Oh, yeah, that's it," he said, his voice louder and bolder now. As if sensing his newfound confidence, the talking in the crowd suddenly subsided and every eye turned towards him.

"Ladies and gentlemen, friends and neighbors, we're here to start a revolution and ... oh, to smeck with it! Here it is. Long live America!"

He strummed the first couple of chords a little tremulously, turned back to the amp and switched the volume higher as Tom and Sol joined in. He could hear his own voice, his own guitar ringing out strong and clear as his confidence and swagger gradually grew with the song's progress. With a fierce joy he saw the crowd begin to react, his pride slowly swelling at his own power over people's spirits as they stared up at him, mesmerized by the music. All his insecurities melted away and his confidence soared. He was floating, flying above the audience, his body buzzing as he saw 1000 ecstatic faces lifted towards him, raised *by* him into emotional bliss. It was beyond anything he'd ever imagined, this feeling, this power to move people! He leaned further into the mike, singing with a passion he'd never felt before as he recited the words Americans had once held dear; words that had been stolen away and almost forgotten under the MeChip's tyrannous hold:

"O! Say can you see by the dawn's early light,
What so proudly we hailed at the twilight's first gleaming,
Whose broad stripes and bright stars through the perilous fight,
O'er the ramparts we watched, were so gallantly streaming?
And the rockets' red glare, the bombs bursting in air,
Gave proof through the night that our flag was still there;
O! Say does that star-spangled banner yet wave,
O'er the land of the free, and the home of the brave?"

As he reached the final note, something happened. A strange sound rippled like a wave over the auditorium, as if an electrical short-circuit had been amplified and repeated a thousand times over.

The crowd was shouting its adulation as the song drew to a close, some cheering his name, before they suddenly stopped. Many put their hands to their necks, as if sensing something wrong.

It had worked, Alex knew it now. The song had worked and the MeChips of every single person in that auditorium had been broken, defeated at last by something so beautiful and rousing it could not contain the emotions it stirred in the human spirit. For all its technological prowess, not even the MeChip could defeat human creativity of this sort, or the feelings it could conjure.

Alex's smiled faded, however, as he looked out at the crowd and saw the beginnings of incomprehension, even fear. Now was the time to explain to them what had happened, to begin to stir them to action, to revolution against their oppressors.

He would need Locke's help, he realized. Scanning the crowd again, he saw his elderly comrade close by now, near the front of the crowd and off to the side.

Then he saw Slade Arnold. The man's eyes were wide as he looked around at the crowd and realized what was happening. Then his face transformed, twisted in fury. As Alex looked on, the traitorous General reached down and pulled a blaster from its holster. A moment later and the weapon was pointing directly at Alex.

Chapter Thirty-Seven
The Beginning

It all happened in an instant. As Alex stood frozen to the spot waiting for the laser blast to strike, someone emerged behind Arnold. Leaping into action, the figure swung a heavy object, smashing it into the back of the General's skull. Arnold's eyes widened in surprise, then closed as he stumbled forward, his fall cushioned somewhat as he collapsed against the massed crowd in front of him and slumped slowly to the ground, unconscious.

When Alex saw his savior, he almost couldn't believe it.

Iggy.

He was holding the same iron bar he'd used to attack Alex earlier. There was a cut on his left cheekbone but otherwise he looked unharmed from his earlier encounter with Sol and the oversized cymbal. He looked at Alex, smiled slightly, and nodded. His old adversary must have realized who the real enemy was. Alex nodded back, feeling gratitude towards Iggy for the first time in his life.

Meanwhile, Alex caught sight of Locke as he stepped forward, took away Arnold's gun, then disarmed the two Fixers, who were standing nearby looking bewildered, as if they had no idea what was going on.

They weren't the only ones. After the crowd's cheers and exultation at Alex's breathtaking performance, the destruction of people's MeChips was starting to make itself felt. Alex realized the crowd would have no idea what was really happening. They would see a suddenly dingy, run-down auditorium, notice their neighbors' now-tattered clothes and sickly faces, find their MeChips no longer working, and then ... what? How, exactly, would they react?

Alex knew he had to do something. But first, he needed to take care of those he loved. Jumping off the stage, he pushed his way through the crowd to his parents, who were looking puzzled and confused. When they saw Alex, they rushed towards him.

"Alex! It's you. I'm so glad you're okay. But what's happening? I had the strangest, most horrible dream ..." his mother began.

"No time for that now," he said, hugging them both. "But you're safe, I promise. Come with me. Let's get you onstage."

He was about to lead them away when he felt a hand on his shoulder. Fearing the worst, he turned back, only to find the thing he wanted most in the world.

It was Abby. She was smiling at him in recognition.

"Hey," she said, her deep brown eyes fixed on his as her fingers slid off his shoulder and her hand found his, gripping it tightly. Alex felt a frisson of excitement and joy as he squeezed her hand in return. But there was little time to enjoy their reunion as he noticed the bruise on her cheek and cut above one eye.

"Abby, are you okay?" he asked anxiously.

"No, but I'll survive," she said, shrugging it off. "And I'm happy to see you in one piece," she smiled. "But I need to know what's going on. I mean, I'm starting to suspect, but I need to know for sure."

"You will. Come with me."

As Alex led Abby and his parents onstage he caught up with Locke, who was heading in the same direction. As he did so, he heard the sound of the audience rise as people turned to their neighbors in confusion. A few started to push their way towards the exits. The whole crowd—1000 people or more—were beginning to panic.

Almost without thinking, Alex rushed towards the microphone, coughed into it, and spoke.

"Listen to me, please!" he said, raising his voice. "I have something important to say. First, don't be afraid! There is a really good explanation for everything you're experiencing. You will be safe if you stay here in this room and listen to me. I promise all will be fine. But you must stay calm!" he shouted, feeling anything but calm himself.

In spite of his own rising panic, his words did the trick. The crowd paused, stopped its jostling and muttering, and turned to face him, waiting for his explanation.

"Nice job, son. I can take it from here," a voice said in his ear.

It was Locke. Up close he looked in pretty bad shape, with blood around the corners of his mouth and more worry lines than Alex remembered ever seeing before. Locke appeared, if anything, at least ten years older for his experience of the last few hours. But his face was set in grim determination as he nodded at his young friend.

Just seeing this clear resolve in Locke's eyes made Alex breathe easier. He sighed, feeling a little of the tension drain away.

"Did we do it, John? Did we win?" he asked.

"We won the first battle, Alex. There will be many more. But we've made a start. The revolution has finally begun."

Alex nodded. He had known that would be Locke's answer even before he asked. This wasn't the end, he knew. It wasn't even the beginning of the end. But they had, at long last, taken the first step. And that was the most important step of all.

"Alright, let me tell the crowd who you are," Alex said, turning back to the microphone and speaking once more to the large audience.

"Ladies and gentlemen, friends and neighbors, let me introduce to you Dr. John Locke, the inventor of the MeChip and the smartest person I know. He will tell you exactly what's going on and—more important even than that—what we plan to do about it!"

THE BEGINNING

About the Author

Chris Spence loves words. From speechwriting to journalism, editing to running environmental organizations, Chris has always sought to connect people and tell stories using the power of language. Originally from the UK, he has since lived in New Zealand, the US and more recently Ireland. He is married with three children and an aged-but-feisty Yorkshire terrier.

Lightning Source UK Ltd.
Milton Keynes UK
UKHW010300071221
395199UK00001B/403